NO BEASTS!
NO CHILDREN!

NO BEASTS!
NO CHILDREN!
Beverly Keller

A Harper Trophy Book

Harper & Row, Publishers

Library of Congress Cataloging-in-Publication Data
Keller, Beverly.
  No beasts! No children!

  Summary: After her mother goes away to find herself,
Desdemona, her father, the twins, and the three dogs learn to
cope by themselves with a strict housekeeper, a heartless
landlord, and an odd aunt.
  [1. Single-parent family—Fiction] I. Title.
PZ7.K2813No 1983   [Fic]   87-45288
ISBN 0-06-440225-8 (pbk.)

First Harper Trophy edition, 1988
Published in hardcover by Lothrop, Lee & Shepard Books

For Ernie and Hal Wiseman

NO BEASTS!
NO CHILDREN!

SHERMAN HELPED US GET READY for the new housekeeper. He watered the weeds and raked over my foot and fell down the back steps with the garbage.

The dogs liked the last part best. They pawed through juice cans and banana peels and rolled in coffee grounds. Then they sat on Sherman and licked his face to thank him.

Sherman is our landlord's son, but animals think of him as just another stray.

I heard our doorbell ring.

The animals raced to the side yard, barking furiously, as if to make up for being a little slow in the watchdog department.

Sherman sat up. "That must be the housekeeper now. Try to make a good impression."

As I limped into the parlor, my father said to a woman standing beside a suitcase, "Mrs. Farisee, this is my daughter Desdemona."

Mrs. Farisee's hair was silver, her eyes the same blue as her soft, shimmery dress and linen pumps.

I had expected somebody plainer. This housekeeper looked like an aunt, retired from an important job, who kept roses on her coffee table and sachets in her closet. I couldn't picture her scrubbing floors, but I could imagine her listening to my problems, offering wise and practical advice, maybe figuring some way to fix my hair so it wouldn't look so lank and weedy.

While my father went out for the rest of her luggage, Sherman sidled into the living room to stare at her.

Ignoring him, she greeted me. "What are you doing in those clothes, Desdemona?"

This did not sound to me like warm, understanding acceptance. "Um . . . wearing them." To change the subject, I brought up Sherman. "This is my friend Sh—"

She was not easily distracted. "Young ladies dress up for guests, Desdemona."

My vision of her brushing my hair and listening to confidences began to waver.

Sherman gazed at her as if she'd dropped out of a bubble from Oz. "Would you like me to take your suitcase?"

She glanced at him. "Not with those dirty hands."

"I think I'll go out with the dogs," Sherman said.

Father came in with two more suitcases, and I went after Sherman.

As he opened the back door the dogs came bounding in, eager to see who was new. They raced over him, across the kitchen, and through the hall to the parlor.

It was too late to stop what I knew would happen.

I could hear Mrs. Farisee getting to know the dogs. "Back! Back, I say! Ugh! *Down!*"

I heard my father roar, "OUT!"

The dogs burst into the kitchen from the hall, now, heading for the back door.

Sherman got to his feet again.

"They hardly scratched your luggage," I heard my father say.

Mrs. Farisee sounded shaken. "Do they slobber all over everybody?"

"Only if some idiot lets them in," my father growled.

"I think I'll go on home," Sherman said.

I was tempted to tag after him, but I already suspected that it would not be wise to risk offending Mrs. Farisee. Besides, after the bedlam I'd just heard, how could I resist seeing what had happened?

When I got to the parlor, Father was picking up the contents of the housekeeper's purse, which were strewn across the room.

"You didn't mention that you had dogs." Her voice sounded cold and dangerous.

Just then, Antony and Aida dashed into the room, skidded, stopped, and stared.

Like most five year olds, they seemed to take a total survey of a stranger—appearance, mind, and character—in a minute's gaze.

Father introduced them to Mrs. Farisee, who asked them how old they were and whether they went to kindergarten yet.

Finally, she turned to Father. "They talk, don't they?"

"Oh, yes," he assured her.

"But mostly to each other," I added.

Antony and Aida glanced at me, then looked at each other as if to say, *Just as I suspected. Nothing there, right? Right. Glad you agree.*

They raced from the room.

"Twins run in our family," I said.

After Father left for work, Mrs. Farisee called Aida and Antony and me into the kitchen and told us how things would be. No running in the house. No dogs in the house. No yelling or barking anywhere. Morning chores, afternoon chores, and an hour's silence after lunch.

She went to her room and unpacked, leaving the twins and me solemn, and me, for one, feeling as if I'd entered a cold, white-tiled tunnel, with no idea where or when it might end.

Just before noon, Sherman returned with a yellow rose for Mrs. Farisee and a brown-bag lunch for himself.

"Thank you." Mrs. Farisee took the rose. "You are not invited to lunch."

"He's never invited," I explained. "He just comes every day."

She looked at him coolly. "Not any more."

Another person would have left, but Sherman just stood waiting.

"All right," she told him, "since you brought your own food, but don't try it again."

Then she chased out the dogs, who had sneaked into the kitchen with the twins.

"This house smells like a kennel," she grumbled as we sat down to eat. "There's hair in the air everywhere."

"I know." Sherman began to unpack his lunch. "I wish I could live here."

"I cannot understand why anybody would put up with three dogs. Take your sleeve out of your soup, Desdemona."

"My mother saved dogs," I explained.

"Lost dogs, stray dogs, sick dogs—her mother saved them," Sherman explained.

I had trouble swallowing the next spoonful. It still happened that something unexpected would suddenly remind me that my mother was a terrific person in a lot of ways.

Mrs. Farisee moved the honey jar just as Aida was about to sweeten her soup. "Your father said your mother was away. Will you be visiting her?"

I tried to answer, but I couldn't get my voice working. I could see the twins starting to get uneasy.

"Their mother left ten months ago. She had to find herself, and she's still working on it." Sherman spoke as if this were natural, nothing for us to be ashamed of. Sherman had never met my mother, but he and I talk a lot.

Even Mrs. Farisee must have seen how uncomfortable the twins and I were. She eased away from the subject, but not entirely. "Did your mother try to find the owners of these dogs, Desdemona?"

"Try? Boy, did she try." Sherman's elbow just missed my glass. "She called everybody. She even advertised, but nobody ever claimed them."

"Maybe it's the class of dogs she saved. From the looks of them, I suspect people lost them on purpose." Mrs. Farisee seized Antony's wrist as he was about to butter his knuckles.

"Then I'm ashamed to belong to the people race." Sherman dropped a macadamia nut.

Mrs. Farisee looked at the food he'd brought—

little rolled sandwiches with pink and green fillings, green olives and tiny onions with toothpicks in them, mixed nuts and petits fours. "Who packed your lunch, Sherman?"

"Our maid."

"Does she always feed you so creatively?"

"These are leftovers. My parents had a party last night."

When we finished doing the dishes, Sherman and I went out to play with the dogs.

Mrs. Farisee's voice split the air like a whip. "Desdemona Blank, come into the kitchen. There are spots on the dishes."

She made me re-wash all the dishes and re-dry them and re-put them away.

I worked fast because of my bottled hostilities. After my mother left us, my father sent me to a psychiatrist. The psychiatrist said I was bottling up my hostilities, and that I should express my anger. Ever since, I've had a nagging vision of my hostilities coming unjugged, a clump of green squishy things exploding out of a container and expanding like bristly, monstrous, ravening genies. I dreaded even the thought of free-raging hostilities, and I certainly didn't want them to break out at Mrs. Farisee in the kitchen now. In a confrontation between the housekeeper and my most ferocious hostilities, I knew I was sure to be the loser.

"Where do you think you're going now?" she demanded when I finished.

"I think I'm going out," I told her honestly.

"We do not wear torn jeans in public."

I was confused, which was better than worrying about berserk hostilities. "Our backyard is public?"

"Your backyard is a disgrace."

I could feel the old hostilities straining against the bottle cork. "It's about the only place our dogs feel welcome lately."

"Dogs are filthy animals. What are you chewing?"

"Gum."

"We do not talk with gum in our mouth. Get rid of it."

I'd been chewing that gum all week. It was just getting ripe.

"Spit it out!" she commanded.

I sacrificed the gum and escaped. Psychiatrist or no psychiatrist, I was relieved that my hostilities had stayed pent-up. That psychiatrist had never met Mrs. Farisee.

"Maybe she's only starting off tough, like the new warden at a bad prison," I told Sherman. "It could be worse."

"How?"

"I was afraid she might be like a mother to us, and make us forget we already have one."

SHERMAN WAS BARELY ELEVEN, blond and pale and skinny, and no good at running or catching or throwing or climbing.

Normally, I would have been embarrassed at having a scraggly little boy for my friend. Not much had been normal, though, since my mother left.

She went away just before the beginning of the school year, which was not the best timing. My father lost weight and sleep and a number of clients. They lost confidence in him when Mother left, since he was a marriage counselor.

Next, *he* started trying to find himself. He grew a beard, told us to call him Mark, wore sunglasses and sandals made from old tires, and meditated. He got furious with anybody or anything that made a sound while he was meditating, so I was enormously relieved when he finally gave it up.

He shaved and invested in contact lenses, new shoes and clothes, and a haircut like the one the sports commentator on the local television news show wore. He got a job selling flashy foreign cars, and traded our old station wagon for a sports car and was out late almost every night. Once he brought a woman to the movies with us. She wasn't much over twenty, with tousled hair and shiny lip gloss and a shirt unbuttoned even lower than his.

It's unnerving to imagine having a stepmother like that while you're still trying to get used to your own mother being gone.

I wondered if all parents who found themselves found somebody their own children couldn't recognize.

When people stopped buying flashy cars, my father got a job as a counselor with a county mental-health clinic in a little town I'd never heard of. We moved there—here—and rented an old two-bed-room house with cracked linoleum floors and a weedy backyard.

We were all edgy and homesick the day we moved in. The dogs trailed the movers nervously. When I put the dogs out back they sat in the weeds, howling, until my father chased them through the house and out the front door.

"The front fence is only a couple of feet tall," I said. "They could jump it and get away."

"Good," he said. "Maybe they'll run off with the kid who's out there watching every move we make."

I knew he didn't mean Antony, because Antony and Aida were standing in the kitchen biting their fingernails and looking haunted.

I went out to be sure the dogs didn't take a notion to jump the fence.

The boy who had been watching every move we made was standing outside the fence looking at the dogs. They sat quietly looking at him; I had the feeling they understood each other.

He was a wispy boy you'd never notice unless he was watching your dogs and someone had just suggested that they might run away with him.

I walked over to the fence and said "Hi" so he'd know I was keeping an eye on him.

He didn't take his gaze off the dogs. "They're big."

I nodded.

"What are they?"

"I don't know. Herb is maybe Old English sheep dog and beagle and Labrador. Joe is possibly collie and Belgian sheep dog and Newfoundland. Sadie may be German shepherd, vizsla, and Gordon setter."

He looked at me. "You know all those breeds of dog?"

"I studied a lot of dog pictures trying to figure what ours might be."

He stared at me as if I'd descended from the clouds in a shower of dog biscuits. "Did you ever see a Catahoula leopard dog?"

"Sure. In pictures."

His eyes shone. "A Queensland heeler? Lhasa Apso? Shar-pei?"

He went on until he ran out of breeds and breath. Then he said, "Want to see my dog pictures sometime?"

"Maybe."

I could see he knew this was less than acceptance, but he hung around. "Could I pet your dogs?"

"I guess so."

He opened the gate, and the dogs stood up as if they'd known him a long time. While he petted them, they licked his face in slow, calm slurps. He shut his eyes and hugged them. He rolled on the dead tan grass with them.

The movers told him to get out of the way.

My father came out and told him to go home. The boy got up and left right away, the dogs looking after him and whimpering softly.

All that day and the next morning we worked, putting things away.

My father told me to water the front yard and get Antony and Aida out from underfoot. When I took them and the dogs out front, the boy was there. I don't know how long he'd been waiting. The dogs ran to the fence and stood on their hind legs to kiss him.

I said "Hi" without enthusiasm, because I suspected he was the kind of kid who'd hang around whether you wanted him to or not.

"Could I give your dogs some leftovers?" he asked.

"What kind?"

He held a cake box over the gate for my inspection. "Ratatouille, artichoke hearts, and crêpes stuffed with raspberry crème. My parents had a party last night." He looked at Antony and Aida, who were hovering over the food. "If you don't want your dogs to eat sweets, we could share the crêpes."

The dogs were perfectly happy with ratatouille and artichoke hearts. The crêpes were otherworldly after a breakfast of cereal and warm milk and "Where the devil are all the plates?" and "Why doesn't the stupid toast pop up before it burns?"

"I hope your mother lets you eat between meals," the boy told the twins nervously.

They walked over to the gate and stared at the man next door. He was trimming the hedge around his front lawn as if it had done something hideous for which he was punishing it.

"They don't talk to most people." I explained Antony and Aida so the boy wouldn't think they were ignoring him because he offended them.

"Did they ever?" With his sleeve he wiped a bit of ratatouille off Herb's nose.

"Oh, sure."

"When did they stop?"

"When our mother left, about ten months ago. She was stifled and she had to find herself." The psychiatrist Father sent me to told me I had to stop avoiding the subject of my mother's leaving.

The boy nodded. He seemed to take her leaving seriously, without acting as if there were something wrong with me.

I was encouraged. "They've improved, sort of. At least now they talk to some people."

The twins, in fact, had become highly selective in their associations. They struck up conversations with sullen ruffians at bus stops. They talked immediately, confidentially, and at great length with panhandlers, derelicts, bill collectors who came to harass my father, and furtive men who peddled genuine Swiss watches for five dollars on the street.

"You must have felt strange when she left." The boy scratched Sadie behind the ears.

"I threw up a lot. And I lost my hair." I began to

feel queasy talking about it, but the psychiatrist said I had to learn to air my feelings.

"All your hair?" He took a burr from between Joe's toes.

"Just a patch at the top. My psychiatrist said it was a stress reaction from rejection."

"Why would anybody reject her own hair?" The boy stood and peered down at my head. "It looks all right now. The hairs are short, but it looks neat, like a new chicken. Anyway, only somebody taller could tell." He sat beside me. "There aren't many kids any size in this neighborhood. The houses are old and small. The original owners live in some, and the rest are rented, and most landlords won't rent to people with children or dogs."

"I guess we were lucky."

"You like the house?"

"My father says it's a dump, but it's the only place where the owner would take dogs and children."

"That's what my father figured. He said your father was so desperate he'd grab anything."

"Your father?"

The boy looked embarrassed. "Harley Grove. It's his house."

"Our landlord?"

"Yeah. I'm Sherman. We thought you had only one dog."

I tried not to look guilty. "My father said we had a dog. That's not really a lie. We do have a dog."

"It would be a good idea not to mention the others. My father was glad to get this place rented without fixing it up, but not glad enough to overlook three dogs. He's not crazy about animals."

I was beginning to feel scared.

"Don't worry about it," Sherman said. "If you pay the rent on time, he won't be around. He's afraid you'll ask him to have the roof repaired."

I was still apprehensive. "How close do you live?"

"Twenty blocks." He looked thoughtful. "Around there, everybody my age is bigger than me and calls me a wimp. Is it okay if I come over tomorrow?"

"We have to go to day care." I was not comfortable trusting anybody who was called a wimp.

"The day care center?"

"No. It was full. This is some lady's house, where I'm sure to be the oldest."

The next evening, Sherman brought the dogs quiche Lorraine and croissants.

While the dogs bolted quiche and the twins munched croissants, I said, "I was right."

"Nobody older?"

"Nobody. Finger paints, tricycles, and dough clay."

"How did the twins like it?"

I could still feel the shame. "The woman who ran it tried to make them talk. Finally, Antony escaped and took off his clothes at the public library. We had to bring everybody in day care to look for him, and we never found his clothes."

"Does he do that often?"

"Only when he's insulted. Aida hummed all day."

"That's not so bad."

"She hummed one note, all day."

The next morning my father advertised for a housekeeper.

"The twins have gone through six day-care places in ten months," I told Sherman, "not to mention Antony's clothes. When I was cleaning the bathroom, I dropped my father's contact lenses down the sink, and last night the man next door complained that our dogs howl when we're gone."

Sherman nodded. "Mr. Troup. He doesn't like dogs or children. That's another reason my father rented you this house. He doesn't like Mr. Troup. Besides, Mr. Troup's daughter Pat is a reporter, and my father is on the City Council. She prints everything he says at meetings. You wouldn't believe some of the dumb things he says."

I was uneasy talking about our landlord. "I hope we get a housekeeper who likes animals. My father says she shouldn't cost more than day care and sitters." I watched Sherman crack walnuts for the dogs. "Sitters. That means he'll be going out every night. Either he's already met some woman, or he's looking."

"What's wrong with that?"

"Can you imagine some girl who goes dancing every night for a mother?"

When I saw my father's advertisement in the newspaper, I knew I had more to worry about than some scatterbrained new mother.

"Wanted. Strong minded, strong willed house-keeper," it began.

My father knew what he wanted. The only trouble was, we got her.

"MRS. FARISEE HATES WILDLIFE," I told my father a few nights after she came. "She vacuumed all my spiders off the ceiling. She kills snails. She is basically a very violent person."

"But a great housekeeper," he observed. "My home has never been so clean and quiet."

"Terror, that's what she uses. Terror and child labor."

"She gets marvelous results," he murmured.

The next morning, after I finished my chores, I sat on the back steps watching Antony and Aida baking a make-believe cake. I almost missed Sherman, who was at his dentist's. At least Sherman talked to me.

Aida shoveled dirt into a pail. "Pretend this is the flour," she told her brother.

"And this is the sugar." He threw in a handful of sand.

Aida picked up the hose. "Now the milk."

After they stirred that mess with their fists, they poured it on the trash can lid to bake.

"You can't leave that mud there," I warned.

They looked at the mud, looked at each other, and decided my advice was not worth acknowledging.

From the kitchen, Mrs. Farisee snapped out, "Lunchtime."

"Better wash up," I told the twins.

Mud up to the elbows, they looked at each other. Agreed that I was not aroused enough to make an issue, they stomped after me into the kitchen.

The housekeeper fixed them with a gaze like a spear. "Out. Wash."

Dazed by the injustice, they stumbled outside, past the dogs waiting to sneak in.

Mrs. Farisee glared at the dogs, who retreated.

The twins returned, almost clean, and ate until they could escape and go out again.

After I finished the dishes, I sat on the back steps.

Aida was smoothing the sand in the sandbox. "This will be the table. We invited the president and the king of Siam and a famous bank robber."

"Desdemona Blank!" Mrs. Farisee called. "Come into the kitchen."

She was waiting for me with a mop. "Do you call this floor clean?"

I still thought there might be a way to establish a relationship with her. "I never call it anything."

She was not amused. "I want it so clean you could eat off it."

This sounded ominous. "Why would I want to do that?"

"Scrub it. And we'll have no more dogs sneaking in."

"If they can't come in, who'll eat off the floor?"

She handed me the mop. "I will be resting in my room, so be quiet."

While I sloshed the mop around, the dogs started barking and yelping outside. If I went out to shush them, I decided, I'd only get in trouble for leaving my work. Besides, I confess I felt an utterly evil satisfaction at having Mrs. Farisee's rest disturbed.

Over the dog's whining, I heard Antony. "There's a horse coming down the driveway."

Aida sounded annoyed. "You can't have a horse eat with the president. If you're going to be dumb, I won't play."

"What kind of horses have stripes?" he asked.

"Not many. Give the king a pail of tea."

"It's looking over your shoulder."

There was a minute's silence. Then Aida said, "That's no horse."

"It looks real," Antony said.

"It's a zebra."

My mother always said the twins were terribly creative. Nobody ever mentioned my being creative. Once, I remember hearing my father tell my mother I was fairly dependable. It made me feel like a used car. Sometimes I wondered if one of the reasons my mother had to go find herself was that I was so dull she needed a challenge.

The dogs were still yipping and crying. I didn't want them to get into real trouble with Mrs. Farisee. Besides, I figured a short break from mopping wouldn't hurt. I went to the back door—then I ran and banged on Mrs. Farisee's door until she opened it.

White stuff like wet glue on her face, pink plastic plugs in her ears, she loomed like Frankenstein's monster glaring down at a peasant. Her glower could have razed a dungeon wall. "*I said I want absolute quiet when I rest.* If you touch my door again, you will be a very, very sorry young lady."

I had no doubt she could think of terrific ways to make me very, very sorry.

I telephoned the SPCA. "Um . . . we have this thing in our weeds that looks like a zebra."

Click.

I telephoned the police. "I think there is a zebra in our garden." I thought people might be slower to hang up on somebody with a garden than somebody with weeds.

"How did this beast get into your flowers?"

"Well, actually, he came to a tea party," I confessed.

"Party?"

"Just a make-believe party."

"All right, missy. I tell you what. You send your make-believe zebra back to his make-believe party and I'll make believe you never called."

I hurried outside.

The dogs were leaping around the zebra. The twins were leaning against its left side, trying to push it out of the sandbox. Stubborn but peaceable, the zebra leaned right back. He was a dark, dusty gray with wide white stripes.

"Stop shoving him," I said. "Maybe we can lead him to somebody who knows the right people to call."

As we went around to his head, I discovered something odd. His right side was solid gray.

When he refused to move, I ran next door. Sherman had said Pat Troup was on a newspaper; I figured somebody would pay attention to her.

Before I got to the Troups' back door, it flew open and Mr. Troup stormed out onto his back stoop. "If you can't shut up those blasted dogs—"

"Mr. Troup, we have what looks like a half zebra in our yard!"

He seemed confused. "Half a zebra in your yard?"

"No, a whole, but half . . . Look over in our yard."

From the stoop we could see over the fence. He peered toward our yard. "Lord have mercy on us!"

We couldn't see much of the creature, with Antony hanging on its neck and the dogs leaping around it and everything deep in weeds, but we could see that the focus of all the action was something big and gray and white.

Mr. Troup dashed into his house. "Find my glasses, quick!"

Through the screen door, I could see the spectacles shoved up on his head. I pointed to them.

Seizing a telephone, he dialed, then shouted, "This is a scoop! Give me Pat Troup!" Putting his hand over the mouthpiece, he snapped at me, "Pull yourself together."

I hiked up my jeans and straightened my shirt.

"Patricia!" he yelled into the telephone. "Don't panic, but there's a beast in the yard next door attacking children. It's . . . it's . . ." He looked at me. "What would you say it is?"

"Well, one side is striped."

"It's striped like a tiger!"

"The other side is solid gray, though."

"Only it's gray, like a wolf!" Hanging up, he told me sharply, "Get hold of yourself. Get a grip on yourself."

I hugged my arms, not wanting to offend him.

"We have to drive it off, if it's not too late already." He rushed out of the kitchen, then came back with a golf club and an umbrella. Handing me the umbrella, he hurried me down the back steps. "You threaten it with that whilst I menace it with the club."

"I don't think we have to scare it."

"Aaaagh!" I heard Aida scream. "It's on my foot!"

"It's got her foot!" We couldn't see over the fence now, but, shoving me aside, Mr. Troup sprinted toward our yard.

I ran after him. "Don't hurt it!"

My voice was lost in a siren's scream. A police car careered into our driveway and slammed to a stop, top light flashing. Two officers leaped out.

"Not me, you fools!" Mr. Troup raged, as the officers tried to wrest the club from him.

A car with a sign reading PRESS on the windshield roared into the drive. A young woman jumped out, followed by a man with a camera. "What are you doing to my father?" she shouted at the police.

Flailing at the officers, Mr. Troup fought his way to our back gate.

There was a howl from Aida. "AIIIIEEE! It stepped on the bank robber!"

Everyone sprang toward the cry. As Mr. Troup struggled to open our gate, the police vaulted the fence and landed among Joe and Herb and Sadie.

Pat Troup and the cameraman leaped into the yard right after the officers.

The dogs jumped on them all, kissing and tripping them. As Mr. Troup came through the gate they wagged and wriggled, despite his threats.

As the police waded through dogs to Aida, neighbors poured into our yard. Pulling plugs from her ears, white stuff like dry concrete on her face, Mrs. Farisee came running out. When she saw the crowd, she ran back in.

As one officer snatched Aida into the air, the other grabbed Antony.

The twins looked at each other as if they were tolerant of this sort of madness, but still found it tedious. They went limp, waiting to be released.

Most of the adults were shouting, a few even crying.

Pat Troup peered at the zebra. Then she turned to her father, her expression much like the twins'.

Everybody was gawking at the animal. Mr. Troup glared at it, then me. The officers put down the twins. The cameraman was laughing.

"Dez!" Wide-eyed and pale, Sherman struggled through the dogs. "What happened? The SPCA is here!"

Joe and Sadie and Herb raced around him, skidding and barking, goofy with excitement.

A woman in a blue SPCA uniform made her way

through the dogs and took turns with the police and the neighbors saying,

I'll be darned.

Craziest thing I ever saw.

Who do you suppose would do a thing like that?

Get down, dog.

The woman turned to Sherman. "Who owns these dogs?"

For a minute, Sherman tried to swallow. Then he nodded toward me. "She owns a dog." He pointed at Antony and Aida. "They own one. Mr. Blank owns one."

"Tell their owners to get them out of here and take them home." She went back to arguing with the police about who got the zebra.

When the officers said they absolutely refused to take it in their patrol car, she gave in. The zebra did not. She and the police had a terrible time getting it into her van.

Neighbors started leaving our yard, most of them laughing. Mr. Troup seized his umbrella from me. "If I ever see you on my property again, girl, I won't be responsible for my actions!"

"Who made the original complaint about the animal?" the SPCA driver asked Pat Troup, who was trying to unhook the press car bumper from the police car bumper.

"My father here called me, then I called you," Pat panted.

"Sir," the SPCA woman told Mr. Troup, "I need some information from you."

"Ask her!" Shaking his golf club at me, he stormed back to his yard.

"Could you come down to the animal shelter?" she asked me. "That van gets hot in the sun."

As Sherman and I went to ask if we could go, Mrs. Farisee, wearing a pink dress, smooth puffy hair, and long glossy eyelashes opened the back door. "Where are the photographers?"

"Finished," I told her, "but I have to go to the animal shelter."

"A suitable place," she snapped.

"Would you come too?" the SPCA woman asked her. "We may need your statement."

Pat Troup drove us to the shelter in the press car.

When we got there, several people were trying to get the zebra out of the van. As soon as the twins slid out of the press car, the animal trotted right out and clomped over to us.

A tanned, strong-looking man with grizzled black hair and a thick black beard came running from the shelter. "Here he is! It's Moriarty!" Rushing to the zebra, he threw his arms around its neck. "You old scoundrel! I've been looking for you all day." He rubbed his beard along its neck. "I suppose you were having yourself a time, you dog."

"Uh, sir," Sherman ventured, "that's not a dog. It's a zebra."

The man squinted down at Sherman. "A what?"

Sherman looked at me. "Isn't it?"

"I'm not sure," I confessed. "Is it?"

The man laughed until tears ran into his beard. Then he said, "This? This is an old sea horse."

"No." I had seen those little spiny things in an aquarium.

Sherman looked dubious, too. "A sea horse?"

The man grinned. "Sea mule, really. I picked him up on my last voyage."

Mrs. Farisee, who had been eyeing everything and everybody with disapproval, uttered her first word since we left home. "Why?"

"Because he was the most miserable, broken down, starved, and mangy animal I ever saw." The man stroked the mule's nose. "I bought him for twelve dollars and brought him home with me."

"On a *boat*?" Sherman asked.

"On my ship. I was captain of the freighter *Orion*. I'm retired now."

"I never saw a striped mule before," I murmured.

The captain smiled. "Did you happen to notice the way he leans against things?"

The twins nodded vigorously.

"He started that on the voyage home, to keep his footing on deck. Now it's his habit. Leaned against my fresh-painted gate this morning until the hinges gave. That's how he got striped and that's how he got loose."

The captain thanked us all and asked our names and where we lived, and led Moriarty away.

When my father heard about the excitement, he was afraid that Mrs. Farisee would quit.

"I am not one to back down from a challenge," she assured him.

I could only pity the challenge.

I AWOKE LATE SATURDAY MORNING. With Mrs. Farisee off, I had a day on my hands and nobody to nag me.

When my mother was living with us, I used to spend Saturdays with my friends. After she left, a lot of my friends seemed to slip away. Of course, I probably wasn't much fun anymore.

Before she went, Mother explained to Antony and Aida and me that she still loved us. I couldn't help wondering, though, how she could go if we were as lovable as she said. I worried that we must have been partly to blame. When my friends started drifting away, I began to suspect there was something deeply and mysteriously wrong with me.

In a way, moving to a new town was a chance to start over as an acceptable person. So far, Sherman thought I was all right, but Sherman was, after all, known as a wimp.

I trudged into the kitchen. Antony and Aida were at the table eating cinnamon toast crusts and giving the centers to the dogs.

Father came in with the mail. "That's what I get for leaving a forwarding address." He tossed a letter on the table. "It's from the relative. She wants to come visit. I'll write and tell her we moved, but I won't tell her where."

I didn't remember the relative very clearly, but anybody seemed to me better than Mrs. Farisee alone. "Don't you want her to visit?"

"I have enough problems without your mother's relative coming."

"Mother always said it was your relative."

"I clearly remember meeting the woman at our wedding. I had never seen her before. She has to be your mother's relative."

"Mother always said she never laid eyes on her before the wedding." I knew this argument by heart from hearing it every time the relative sent a letter or a gift or card.

"She gave us that blasted toaster that never works. She is part of your mother's family."

"Mother said it was the coffeepot that always

boils over." I could see the old argument was upsetting him. "Why don't we ask the relative who she is?"

Father looked reproachful. "I couldn't ask her after all these years. I'd feel like a fool."

"Can she come?"

"Where would we put her?"

"We could put her in the pantry. It's a big pantry." We had no other space. Antony and Aida and I shared one small bedroom, and Mrs. Farisee had a smaller one, and my father slept on a sofa-bed in the parlor.

"Not a bad idea. If I write that the only space we have is in the pantry, she'll have the sense not to come." He showed me the signature on the letter she'd sent. "Is that Marta or Maria?"

"You don't remember?"

"It's been years, and she's not that memorable."

"What did I call her?"

"Aunt." He peered at the return address on the envelope. "Can you make out the last name?"

"It looks like Van . . . Van . . ."

"I'll just scrawl something that approximates it. At least the address is legible. What's the matter?"

It bothered me that he could be so offhand about rejecting somebody. "Why don't you like her?"

"It's not a matter of liking. She'd be one more thing to contend with."

The telephone rang and he answered it. I could tell by the way his voice deepened that he was talking to a woman, and, in spite of myself, I got uneasy. I wanted him to be happy, and not tense and harassed, but I couldn't find it in me to welcome a rival to my own mother, not even someone who might replace Mrs. Farisee.

That night my father wrote Aunt. As he stamped the envelope, he said, as if to justify himself further, "Besides, she's odd."

Odd she was. She wrote back that she'd love to come, that the pantry sounded cozy.

Mrs. Farisee wasn't pleased by the prospect of an aunt in the pantry. She went out of her way to invent miserable jobs for us. When she ran out of wretched chores, she had me wash the outside of the front windows while the twins washed the inside.

As I turned the hose on the panes, Antony and Aida shrieked and leaped. We were making the best of our work when Sherman came into the front yard. I kind of turned the hose a little bit his way, and he more or less walked into the water. Then he sort of nudged the bottom of the ladder, so the hose and I landed in an old oleander bush.

I didn't notice the taxi until I heard a man say, "Hey, lady. You forgot to pay me."

"Oh."

This sounded more interesting than grappling for the hose, so I said, "Cut it out, Sherman."

"Hey, lady," the man said again, "don't you want your suitcase?"

"Oh. Yes."

I turned the hose off and peered out from under the lemon tree. "It's the relative, all right."

My memories of her were fuzzy, but this could be nobody else. She was slightly overweight and her hair, short, brown, and curly, looked as if it had been cut by somebody while sneezing.

She bent down and picked up what looked like a fat but ratty piece of fur.

As she lifted it, the fur moved.

It slithered up her arm, crept to her shoulder, collapsed against her, and went dormant.

"That's the laziest cat I ever saw," observed the driver, setting her suitcase on the sidewalk.

"He may just be finding it hard to put up with things," the relative said.

She carried her suitcase to our front gate, stopped to open the gate, and set the suitcase down on her foot. As she opened the gate, her purse came unfastened and things spilled out of it.

I realized that Mrs. Farisee would have something to say about my greeting the relative soaking wet. I grabbed Sherman's arm, and we crept around to the side of the house.

As we climbed through the kitchen window into

the sink, the doorbell rang. I heard Mrs. Farisee's steps, like the advance of the Prussian army.

While Sherman sneaked out the back door, I hurried to my room.

Sherman is no good at sneaking. I heard a rush at the back door, whines, whimpers, the scramble of paws. Before the dogs could be intercepted, I heard the relative meeting them. "Oh, dear. Oh, my! Oh, no!"

Then, *"Reeoooowrrr!"*

I ran to the parlor. That cat had come in with the relative. He was on her head, legs stiff under him, back arched, tail and hair like a forest of exclamation marks. From the looks of the relative, he'd scrambled right up her. She was standing on a coffee table, the dogs bounding and grinning and wagging their tails at her and the spitting cat.

Mrs. Farisee made herself heard over the uproar —easily. Even the cat cringed. The dogs trembled. Rolling their eyes, bellies dragging the rug, they crawled for the hall.

Silent, like critics watching a moderately interesting play, the twins stood by the window.

Before Mrs. Farisee could turn her attention to me, I fled.

Crawling over three beds, I reached our closet, changed, climbed out the bedroom window, and hurried back to the front yard.

A minute later, Mrs. Farisee came out and told

me to put on something respectable, come greet my aunt, and make it clear that cats were not welcome in the house.

When I got to the parlor, Aunt was sitting on the sofa, the cat stretched limply across her lap.

He was so still, I was scared. "How is he?"

"Fine, but he's had a shock," Aunt said. "Dogs . . . dogs came in. You know, I didn't remember you had dogs."

"I don't think we did, last time you visited us."

"Thank goodness. I couldn't understand how I could have forgotten them. They don't seem to get along very well with your cat."

"It's not our cat," I said.

The cat opened his eyes and looked at me, unblinking.

For the next few days, Mrs. Farisee stalked around giving Aunt short shrift and shorter answers and making sharp comments about having extra responsibilities thrust on her. Aunt tried to help by doing the cooking, which only made Mrs. Farisee more snappish.

The cat made up his mind that he lived with us. He was constantly slipping around some unwary person, or through a loose screen. This made the dogs more determined to get in, and now and then they did. There would be a scene, the cat streaking up curtains or persons, the dogs wild with excitement, until Mrs. Farisee descended. In an instant, from their *Whoops! Whoopee! Riot!* it was *Oh, Lord. Oh, no. We did it again. Crime. Punishment. Horror. Sin. The world's in ashes. Grovel.*

Aunt bought the family a food processor. It went berserk the first time she used it, shooting out jets of waffle batter until Father shut off all the electricity in the house. He left for work without breakfast and without saying good-bye. I noticed he was wearing his shirt unbuttoned one more button, and I wondered whether he had his eye on some woman already, or was thinking about going out looking again.

Aunt took the food processor back where she got it. The rest of us were finishing lunch when the cat slipped in with Sherman, and the dogs charged in behind. The cat climbed Mrs. Farisee. By the time we got all the animals out, her voice was like steel slivers. "That cat has got to go."

"It doesn't have anywhere to go," Sherman protested.

"If you're so worried about it, you take it," she challenged.

"I'm not allowed." He looked nervous. "My parents don't want hair on the furniture."

"What would they say if they knew the Blanks had three dogs here?" she demanded.

"I don't know. I'll never tell them," he vowed.

"His father never comes over," I said. "He doesn't want to fix the roof."

"Don't worry," Sherman told the twins, who were beginning to look edgy. "Nobody's going to rat on your dogs."

He took the cat around the neighborhood to see if anybody would adopt it. The twins were out back and I was doing the dishes when Mrs. Farisee observed, "It's quiet out there."

That line is in almost every jungle movie or western I've ever seen. The tribal drums have been beating all day, and the young or unstable explorer or cavalryman has gotten hysterical, screaming, "Drums! Drums! Drums!" until the wiser explorer, or sergeant, settles him down, usually by slugging him, and explains, "So long as you can hear the drums, you know those devils aren't attacking. It's when the drums stop that you have to worry." Night falls, and the explorers or cavalrymen have made camp, when one of them says, "It's quiet outside," and the older one says, "Too quiet!" *and you realize the drums have stopped. . . .*

I ran out back.

The twins were digging a hole, with a lot of dog help. Even with all the weeds, I could see that hole would be hard to overlook.

"It's got to be big enough for all the dogs?" Antony asked Aida.

"And us, too," she said.

"Us?" He sounded nervous.

"If we're not in there with the dogs, who'll save them if somebody puts the rat on them?"

Suddenly, the dogs left digging and raced to the gate. It was Sherman, so upset that they crowded around him, looking up at him and whining and licking his face.

"The l . . . the l . . . the landlord is coming!" he stammered.

"What?" For a moment, I didn't understand him.

"My father's almost here!"

Antony and Aida looked at the hole. I understood, then.

Sherman and I were herding the dogs into the house when the doorbell rang. "Hide them!" I whispered, and hurried to get to the door ahead of Mrs. Farisee.

Sherman's father was tall and tanned, with thick blond hair and aviator sunglasses; he looked like somebody in an advertisement for men's cologne.

I tried to tell myself he could have come for some perfectly friendly reason. "Good aftermorning, Mr. Groove."

Sherman came in and sat on the sofa, grinning like somebody caught in the middle of a disgusting criminal act.

Mr. Grove's eyes were difficult to see through his sunglasses. "Is Mr. Blank home?"

"Oh, no." I forced myself to speak calmly. "He wags . . . I mean, works."

"You know, when you moved in, your father said you had a dog. A dog." Mr. Grove was stern.

"Would you like a cup of tea?" I could think of nothing to do but escape to the kitchen and call my father.

"What was that barking?" Mr. Grove asked.

"A cookie?" I suggested, feeling shifty and disreputable.

"Something is whining," he said.

"Pound cake," I quavered. "I think we have some pound cake."

One of the dogs howled.

"What is that?" Mr. Grove demanded.

"Toast!" Sherman stood on the sofa. "She makes a great piece of toast!"

Aunt came in the front door. "I got my money back for that horrible machine." She smiled at Mr. Grove. "Oh. Hello."

The hall door opened and Mrs. Farisee backed into the parlor. "Down! Back! Back, I say!" Turning, she greeted Sherman's father. "I see someone let you in. I'm Mrs. Farisee."

He nodded, rather like a duke acknowledging the crowds. "I'm Harley Grove."

"The landlord," Sherman added.

Mrs. Farisee glanced at me. "Desdemona, do go

wash your face, but watch out for the dog in the bathroom."

Edging out of the parlor, I fell over Aida, who was dragging Joe away from the door. I hurried into the bathroom, splashed my face, led Sadie into my room, and hurried back to the parlor before Mrs. Farisee could make things worse.

As I entered, Sherman's father scowled. "Something howled."

"Lemonade," I said. "Would anybody like a glass of lemonade?"

"I'd be glad to put on some coffee," Mrs. Farisee offered, "if someone would get that dog out of the kitchen."

"Dez," Sherman asked, "could I speak to you a minute?"

I followed him into the hall. "Listen," he whispered, "I'll keep the dogs quiet. You go back there and remind him about the faucets that leak and the windows that don't open and all the other things wrong with the house. When tenants start to complain, he usually leaves."

The door to the parlor opened. "Sherman," Mr. Grove said, "what are you whispering . . ."

There was a clatter of paws as the dogs came rushing to meet Mr. Grove.

The twins helped me pull them off him, and Mrs. Farisee shouted, "Out, you brutes!"

Aunt brushed off Mr. Grove's jacket. "My. They really took a liking to you."

Sherman beamed hopefully. "Aren't they great?"

Mr. Grove picked up the remains of his sunglasses.

"We're taking good care of your house," I told him. "We keep everything clean." I felt sick and shaky.

"Not perfect," Sherman said, "but clean."

"Your father said you had a dog." Mr. Grove's gaze was steely. "But three dogs and three children tearing up this place—that's too much. I've had a complaint about your having so many animals. As a city councilman, I can hardly rent to people who lower property values."

"What he means," Sherman told us, "is that Mr. Troup is threatening to call him a slumlord at City Council meetings again."

"You keep out of this," his father snapped.

"They can't *move!*" Sherman protested.

Mr. Grove was cold. "They certainly can. In sixty days, unless they get rid of the dogs."

"Don't you have any feelings?" Aunt demanded.

"I'm in real estate," he said.

When Mr. Grove left, Aunt and Sherman and I sat on the back steps with the twins.

"Maybe we should talk to Mr. Troup," Aunt suggested.

"I don't think he'd let us on his property." I remembered him shaking the golf club at me.

"Besides," Sherman added, "my father has probably found another desperate family who'll pay even more rent for this dump. I don't know why I put up with him. He wouldn't even look at the cat —just told me to get it out of our house. I'd come live with you, but I'd only be evicted in sixty days."

SHERMAN AND THE TWINS AND I were sitting out front with the cat, who had taken over the porch railing as his private territory, when the sea captain, Langley Morris, strode up the walk with red roses and four packages. He rang our bell while we unwrapped the parcels—catcher's mitt, catcher's mask, softball, and roller skates.

Mrs. Farisee opened the door and accepted the roses and invited the captain in for tea. She told us to stay out.

Sitting on the front steps, I told Sherman, "Wouldn't it be wonderful if the captain would find Mrs. Farisee so irresistible that he'd take her out of our lives?"

"On the other hand," Sherman observed, "he seems like a nice man."

We could hear Mrs. Farisee chatting with the captain in the parlor.

She told him he shouldn't put sugar in his tea if he wanted to keep his weight down.

She asked him if he didn't think he'd look nicer without his beard.

She said she couldn't understand how anybody would want to keep a mule unless he was going to work it.

A few minutes later, Moriarty came visiting, right through Mr. Troup's front yard. Mr. Troup charged out of his house, waving a golf club and yelling hideous threats. As Moriarty trotted toward us, rolling his eyes, the captain and Mrs. Farisee came running out of our house, followed by Aunt.

"This is a residential neighborhood," Mr. Troup shouted. "If you think you can bring mules—"

"Now, what is this mule doing to you?" The captain put an arm over Moriarty's neck.

"If the blasted thing is yours, keep it home!" Mr. Troup snarled.

The captain's eyes narrowed. "How I keep him is my business."

"Not if he's trampling other people's yards," Aunt observed mildly.

The captain glared at her. "Did anybody ask you?"

"Mind your tongue, you rotter," Mr. Troup snapped.

"Please!" Mrs. Farisee implored. "Think of the neighbors."

"If you can't care for your mule properly, you shouldn't have him," Aunt told the captain.

"This mule, madam, is none of your affair," he growled.

Aunt's face got pink and she squinted fiercely. "I should turn you in to somebody."

Sherman's eyes got enormous. "To who?"

"To *whom*," Mrs. Farisee corrected him.

"Can she do that?" Sherman asked me. "Can she turn him into somebody else?"

"If there's ever the slightest hint you don't treat this animal properly, I will turn you in to the SPCA," Aunt warned the captain, and stalked into the house.

"Oh, wow!" Sherman stared after her.

Saying good-bye to everyone but Mr. Troup, the captain led Moriarty away.

"I'm glad he's still himself," Sherman said.

Mr. Troup went into his house and came out with a pair of pruning shears to behead our flowers. I'd seen him do it before—he decapitated any of our blossoms that nosed over his hedge. Instead of throwing them in the trash this time, he brought them to our front door.

As I watched, speechless, he rang our bell. When Aunt opened the door, he handed her the flowers.

"I'm your next-door neighbor, but we've never been properly introduced."

She actually invited him in.

"Everything is turning out all wrong," I told Sherman.

"Of course."

"What do you mean, 'of course'?"

"Murphy's Law," he said.

"What do you mean, 'Murphy's Law'?"

"Murphy's Law says 'If anything can possibly go wrong, it will.'"

"Where did you learn that?" I demanded.

"I read it. In a bitter book."

When my father got home, Aunt and I told him about Mr. Grove's ultimatum. We'd agreed not to tell him we thought Mr. Troup had ratted on us. I was afraid Father would go over and express his feelings to Mr. Troup, and I had seen Mr. Troup's temper.

The news made Father grim and depressed. After dinner, as we sat in the parlor, I realized he couldn't even go to bed until everyone else did. I felt so sorry for him I ached—he had no room of his own, a wife who had to leave him to find herself, three children who didn't look as if they'd ever find themselves, three dogs nobody else wanted, a houseguest he didn't want, and a housekeeper his children didn't want. I wondered if he felt like a total failure, especially having been a marriage counselor. It is not a question you ask your father.

"I don't know how we're going to find another house," he said the next morning at breakfast. "I must have looked at every vacant house in this town before we moved here, and there's nothing for a family with even one dog."

"You're going to have to get rid of those animals," Mrs. Farisee told him.

"How?" Aunt demanded. "Dump them at the pound? Mrs. Farisee, how would you like to be locked in some cage, abandoned?"

I could see that the idea appealed to the twins.

My father started looking again for a place to live.

Since children seemed less welcome than hired killers or motorcycle gangs in rental housing, I didn't offer to go with him. Alone, he could at least get in the door, and if he made a splendid impression, he could mention that he had a child. If that didn't get him kicked out instantly, he could gradually let it be known that he had three, and finally ease the conversation around to dogs.

Whenever he wasn't working, he looked for houses, coming home so quiet that there was no need to ask what luck he'd had.

Every day I got more scared. I couldn't talk about the fear because that would make it seem more substantial.

When Mrs. Farisee mentioned giving up our dogs, my father didn't answer. If he could find no place open to a family with dogs, though, would he at some point think about being a family without them? He'd given no hint that he had ever considered parting with Sadie or Joe or Herb, but a man with children who lose hair and stop talking knows better than to stir things up.

Besides, if adults can leave their children, who can be sure they won't give up a dog?

I talked to Joe and Sadie and Herb more than usual and brushed them until they buried the brushes. In dreams, now, I was always searching alleys and swamps and pounds for them.

Finally, I volunteered to go house hunting with my father. I think I felt that being with him, I could recognize and ward off any dreadful idea that might assail him.

The twins didn't want to come, out of a simple, childlike fear that Mrs. Farisee might somehow get put in a cage when they weren't there to observe. It was a relief not to have to worry about Antony getting insulted right in the middle of somebody's rental house.

My brother taking off his clothes might have gotten us rejected faster, but no firmer. We were turned down everywhere at the first mention of dogs, before my father got a chance to explain what good and deserving beasts ours were.

"Rejection makes you feel rejectable, even when you try to tell yourself you're not." Riding home, I felt grubby and unworthy and so insecure that I had to bring up the dogs. If I didn't know what was on his mind, how could I hope to change it? "If you didn't have Antony or Aida or me, you wouldn't have the dogs, and you could live anywhere."

"A dog is not a toy to be outgrown and dumped. Only trash get rid of dogs when they become inconvenient."

That was as solid a reassurance as I could have asked, but even then I had to test it. "I guess your life would be a lot easier without us."

"What would I be without you? Just another dashing, devil-may-care, irresistible macho adventurer you see in after-shave commercials. Imagine what it would be like to watch those commercials hour after hour, every day and night."

"I never thought about it."

"Then think what it would be like to *be* those commercials hour after hour, every day and night."

Not every father can be that reassuring with class. At my age, of course, you don't accept everything a parent says without question. It's a matter of principle. "Mr. Grove looks like one of those commercials."

"A lot of us try to *look* our fantasies, Dez, even

to live them now and then, or for a time. Grove has Sherman and work and probably a wife to keep him rooted in three dimensions."

"Roots hold you down."

"Roots connect you to the world."

The next week we got invitations to Pat Troup's wedding; one to Mark Blank, one to Felicia Farisee, one to Martha Vandendorf. At last we learned who Aunt was, or at least what her name was.

"Mr. Troup invited them because of Aunt," I told Sherman. "He comes over every day to see her."

Sherman wiped mud off Herb's nose.

"Sherman, he would never have had the nerve to send wedding invitations if he had ratted on us."

"I know." Sherman brushed dead grass off Joe's chin.

"That means somebody else told your father about our dogs."

"I know." Sherman picked a burr from Sadie's fur. "It could have been Mrs. Farisee or it could have been anybody, Dez. You'll feel better if you keep reminding yourself it could have been anybody."

Father was too busy house hunting to be interested in weddings. "I don't even *know* a Pat Troup."

Aunt went right out to buy a gift. She came

home with a miniature television set from a discount house clearance sale. "I want to get people elegant things," she confided, "but I never have the money. I end up buying off-brands at tacky stores. But this looks like a good little set. It's battery operated, so it can go anywhere."

I was nervous the day of the wedding. "Are you sure the twins and I were included in my father's invitation?" I asked Aunt.

"It didn't say 'no children,' so children must be welcome," she assured me. "Besides, nobody whose daughter is getting married notices the guests. Everybody will be paying attention to the bride and groom. Weddings are wonderful—music and a buffet and crying, maybe even dancing."

My father went out before the rest of us started getting ready for the wedding. It was just as well.

Mrs. Farisee styled her wiglet in the bathroom and left it in there. When Aida bathed, somehow it fell into the tub. Antony went in to take his bath, and thought it was something that had drowned. If they hadn't stuck a little marker of popsicle sticks over its grave, we might never have found it.

Aunt told Mrs. Farisee that it was unfair to keep the twins home, and Mrs. Farisee stormed to her room. I stopped Aunt from pursuing her. "If you and she keep fussing, nobody will get to the wedding. Besides, she's got the twins so unstrung that Antony is apt to take his clothes off at any time, on the slightest provocation. Since Mrs. Farisee's in her room, the twins will get to watch a movie on television with the sound off, which they'd prefer to any wedding." I didn't tell her they'd be watching a horror movie. I knew they would because nobody ever allowed them to watch horror movies.

By now, Aunt was so confused that she rushed to get ready. Even so, we were too late to wrap the television set. She put it under her arm and stuck the gift paper in her purse. When we got to the church, the wedding was beginning, so she told me to go in and take a seat while she stayed in the foyer to wrap the gift.

The church was fairly crowded, but I slipped into a pew and tried to look as if I felt welcome.

The minister had already begun to talk. It was solemn and nice. I wondered what my parents had thought about when they got married.

As the groom put a ring on Pat's finger, a woman's voice rang through the church. "What is that landing on the grass?"

A number of people craned around, then turned back, remembering their manners.

The minister glanced up, then collected herself. "I now pronounce you—"

From the back of the church came a man's voice. "There's a door opening on the side!"

More people turned this time.

The minister looked up, then continued, "—pronounce you husband—"

"They're monsters! Armed monsters!" The woman's voice again.

"—and wife," the minister said firmly.

The woman's voice was suddenly louder. "Run! Run for your life!"

Guests scrambled over pews, dashing for the exits. Swept out with them, I was seized by a hedge. As the guests scattered, their cries dwindling into the twilight, and as I struggled to free my left foot, I heard swooshing noises and a *blip-blip-blip* coming closer; then, "Desdemona?"

"Aunt! *Help!*"

She put down the set, which was blaring screams, shots, and explosions, and helped me free my foot.

"What did you *do*?" I cried.

"It went on when I tried to wrap it, and it won't turn off."

"Leave it." I was terrified that a wedding guest would catch us. "Just leave it."

She picked up that squalling machine.

We'd run almost to our house when a car screeched to a stop beside us and Mr. Troup leaned out. "Take cover!"

"Nothing can stop them! Call the Pentagon!" the set bawled.

Mr. Troup stared at it, then at Aunt. "You! *You!*"

She and I hurried up the porch steps and into the parlor. As I shut the door firmly behind us, Langley Morris, sitting beside Mrs. Farisee on the sofa, stood.

Our front door shivered under a succession of blows. The dogs came barking into the parlor, followed by the twins.

Then I heard my father's voice, outside. "I'll thank you to stop abusing our door."

And, unmistakably, Mr. Troup: "I want that monster out here!"

"You are not going to intimidate any of my children until I hear what happened." Father was loud and firm.

"What happened?" Mr. Troup yelled. "What happened? That woman turned a nine-thousand-dollar wedding into a madhouse."

"It's the end of civilization!" The voice on the television almost drowned out the captain's crisp "Turn off that blasted set!"

"That's the whole problem." Aunt fumbled with buttons and levers. "It won't turn off."

"I'm calling the police!" Mr. Troup roared.

Our front door opened and my father hurried in, carrying a grocery sack and accompanied by a blond woman in a red dress. "What is going *on* here? He closed the door behind them. "Turn down that television!"

"It's stuck," I told him.

"Get a screwdriver," he said.

"I'd better head off Troup before he calls the law." The captain went outside.

"You won't want to hear this," Mrs. Farisee told the twins. "Desdemona, help me get them to bed."

The blonde followed us. "Where is your ladies' room?"

From the kitchen, Aunt called, "Where do you keep the screwdrivers?"

Outside, we could hear Mr. Troup and the captain talking. They were louder than the television, and almost as vehement.

Leaving the twins to Mrs. Farisee, I pawed through kitchen drawers with Aunt until we found a screwdriver. By the time we brought it to Father, his face was red and he talked with his teeth clenched. As he struggled with the television set, it crackled and screeched.

The blonde came back to the parlor wearing a fresh layer of lip gloss. "Is *Dance Fever* over yet?"

Aunt knelt beside Father. "Get the batteries out. That's the only way to stop it."

He hit the top of the set. "I can't *find* the stupid batteries!"

"It's easier to just change the channel," the blonde observed.

"This is the end of mankind!" squawked a wavy, purple-faced apparition on the television screen.

"That tears it." Father stood. Something had,

indeed, torn him. "Where do you buy this *junk*?"

Before Aunt could respond, I said, "Let me get bandages."

As I hurried back to the parlor with the first-aid kit, the blonde was trying to wrap father's hurt finger in wedding paper. Mrs. Farisee was yelling out the window for the captain to think of the neighbors. Sadie wet on the rug, and Herb and Joe began to howl. The twins were close behind me.

Father opened the kit. "Ugh!"

I glared at the twins. "What are you doing filling our first-aid kit with mud cakes?" Then I remembered I had told them not to bake mud on the trash can lid.

Aunt attacked the television set with the screwdriver. Holding wedding paper around his cut finger, Father kept snapping directions at her. As the faces on the screen turned from green to violet, Aunt snapped back at Father. The figures on the set got tall and wavy, and Father said, "For heaven's sake, not that way," and Aunt said, "Well, at least I'm not gashing myself," and the screen filled with colored flakes. Finally, Aunt pried off a panel at the back of the set and took out the batteries.

The captain came in. "Nobody can talk to that man."

"I have to apologize to him." Aunt started for the door.

The captain took her arm. "I wouldn't do it just now. He says if you ever show your face in this town again he'll have you tarred and feathered."

The thought seemed to cheer my father.

"Why don't we get something to eat?" the captain asked Aunt. "I don't imagine the wedding reception was too successful."

"It didn't even start," I said.

"I thought you and I were going to have a quiet supper here alone," the blonde told my father.

Mrs. Farisee looked at her as if she were one of the twins on a bad day. "Antony and Aida and I have eaten," she said icily.

The captain took Aunt and me and the cat to a drive-in restaurant. The cat came because it was lying on our porch railing as we left the house, and the captain remarked on what an extraordinarily calm animal it was, and I told him it was a stray, so the captain brought it along.

The captain parked in the back row of cars at the drive-in so that Aunt wouldn't have to show her face. "I really did it," she said. "I broke up a wedding and your visit to Mrs. Farisee."

"I wasn't visiting her," he said. "I came to see you."

"Me? Oh." She was quiet for a minute. "And I almost got you into a fight with Mr. Troup. How can I make it up to the Troups? How can I give Pat her present?"

"You seem to have a lot of trouble with wedding gifts," I observed.

"I have trouble with all machines," she said. "I'll have to buy Pat something else. I still have a little money in my credit union at work."

"What kind of work do you do?" Langley Morris held a cup of milk for the cat.

"I'm a computer programmer."

As the cat settled down in his lap, the captain said, "I think I'll name him Baskerville. He needs a dignified name."

On the way home we drove past the Odd Fellows Hall. Pat's wedding reception was going on, loud and crowded.

"That's a lovely thing about humans," Aunt said, looking less miserable. "They're hard to discourage for long."

THE NEXT SATURDAY MORNING Mr. Troup put a sign on his fence: GARAGE SALE.

"Do you suppose he's selling his house because of us?" I asked Aunt. "Just before we moved here, we had a garage sale."

"Why would he move because of us?" Father asked. "He only has to hold out six weeks and we'll be gone."

I was uncomfortable when my father sounded cool and cynical.

Every day it seemed more and more likely that we would find no place to live, and be like families you see on television, forced to live in their car. Somehow, an entire family forced to live in a sports car didn't even seem pathetic.

Blank's Law: When it seems as if nothing worse

could happen, you can count on something worse happening.

"I love garage sales," Aunt confessed now, "but I don't even dare take a wedding gift over there."

"That's ridiculous," Father said crisply. "Troup isn't going to hold a grudge over a couple of silly misunderstandings."

I pictured Mr. Troup brandishing a hairy, snarling grudge while two misunderstandings giggled and grinned up at it.

"Will you come?" Aunt asked me.

"I have to wash my hair."

"That's just an excuse," Father told me sternly. "You have to learn to face irrational fears, Desdemona. Troup is not going to drive away customers from his garage sale."

"Will you come with us?" I asked him.

"I have to mow the lawn," he said.

"I'll mow it if you'll come with us," I offered.

"I have a lot of things to do," he told me firmly.

"I guess you're scared, too," I murmured.

"That is nonsense. If I wanted to go to that garage sale, I'd be over there in a minute."

"We'll come with you," I said.

"Are you afraid to go by yourself?" he demanded.

"Yes," I admitted. "I'm glad you're not."

Aunt couldn't muster the courage to come with us, but I was stuck. I had to show my father that if he could be mature and face his fears, I could face mine.

When he and the twins and I strolled into the garage next door, Mr. Troup greeted us. "If you're here to make trouble, I'll throw you out before you make a move."

"We are here," my father informed him with great dignity, "as potential customers. You cannot advertise a public sale and then turn people away."

Mr. Troup's eyes narrowed. "It may be a public sale, but you're on private property."

The other people in the garage went on rummaging through dented pots, chipped ashtrays, cannisters, and curtain rods. As Father and Mr. Troup snarled about lawyers and civil rights, Antony plunged into a clutter of broken roller skates and Aida pawed through a jumble of old books.

I took my father's hand. "Why don't we go home?"

He looked down at me. "We have a perfect right to be here. Take your time and look around. Enjoy."

"If you touch anything," Mr. Troup warned me, "I'll have you arrested."

Antony stepped between them, holding a thing by its neck. Its head was made of china, the scalp dotted with tiny holes but bare of hair. Its one blue eye rolled around like a demented ghoul's, the rubber band that kept it in the head visible through the empty socket. Between its simpering parted lips were a few tiny teeth and more broken ones. This head was sewed onto a dirty gray cloth body which hung limp and lumpy from my brother's fist. Looking at Father, Antony lifted it higher.

"It's a doll," Father said absently. "At least, it was."

"He wants it," I said.

"You don't want that," Father told him.

"If you're not going to buy it, put it down," Mr. Troup snapped at Antony.

Antony clutched the doll to his chest.

"You'd better be careful," I warned Mr. Troup. "He takes his clothes off when he's insulted."

"You don't want that old thing," Father told Antony again.

Antony squeezed his eyes shut until his face purpled.

"I knew you just came to make trouble," Mr. Troup accused Father. "If you're too cheap to buy your own son a miserable two-bit doll . . ."

"I can buy my son any miserable two-bit doll he wants."

Antony opened his eyes to follow the argument.

"All right. How much is your miserable two-bit doll?" Father took out his wallet.

"Ten dollars."

"You're out of your mind."

"That doll is a genuine antique. It belonged to Patty's great-grandmother."

"She didn't take very good care of it," I noted.

"Ten cents," Father said.

"Eight dollars," snapped Mr. Troup.

Antony looked from one to the other, his mouth open so he wouldn't lose time if he decided to scream. Father and Mr. Troup yelled numbers at each other. Finally Father handed Mr. Troup a dollar and told him he was a bandit.

Aida grabbed Father's sleeve and held up a book.

"I am not going to pay one cent for *A Guide to Sewage Treatment in Rural Areas*." Shoving the book at Mr. Troup, Father seized Aida by the hand and stalked out of the garage.

"At least no son of mine ever played with dolls," Mr. Troup yelled after us.

Father took us downtown and bought Aida a picture book. She wouldn't look at it.

He offered to trade Antony any toy on the counter for the doll. Antony clutched it tighter.

Father bought me a puzzle and took us for sodas.

Aida stared at the table, tears running down her face. Antony patted the doll's grimy ear.

"Do you ever have days when you feel like a total failure?" Father asked me.

"A lot." I felt closer to him than I had for a long time.

When we got home, Aunt was repairing the front fence. "Ugh. What's that?" she greeted us.

"Pat Troup's great-grandmother's doll," I said.

Antony held it up for her to admire. "Poor thing," she murmured. Then she smiled at me. "Aren't you glad you went to the garage sale? I knew it would be fun."

"Antony gives me the creeps," I told Aunt. "He and Poor Thing."

"Poor Thing?"

"That doll. It *dangles* as if all its bones are missing."

"I don't believe dolls have bones."

"You know what I mean. That vacant eye, and the other rolling around, and all the holes in its scalp."

"Think of them as hair roots. That doll probably had a beautiful head of real human hair. Each strand was knotted and drawn through a hole. It was a marvelous doll in its day."

"Well, it's a horrible sight in our day. And Antony carries it everywhere."

"Boys need to love things as much as girls do."

"I know, but it's driving my father crazy."

"Your father isn't silly enough to think that only girls should play with dolls."

"Maybe. But it makes him nervous."

Father's voice came from out back. "How about a game of catch?"

I looked out the window. Antony was sitting in the sandbox rocking Poor Thing. Aida put down a pail and ran to Father.

"Hey, son! How about a game of keep-away?" Father called.

Antony fed Poor Thing a little sand and wiped her mouth.

"Race you to the corner, boy!" Father challenged.

Aida hunkered down for the signal. Antony peered into Poor Thing's eye socket.

"Anybody want to go house hunting?" Father asked. I could tell he didn't mean me.

Antony dragged Poor Thing past him, to our room.

"Your father is trying to relate to you," Aunt told him.

Shaking the sand out of Poor Thing's head, Antony put her in the box he'd fixed for a crib.

When Father got home from house hunting, Aunt tried to relate to him. "It's important for boys to be loving and gentle, Mark."

"I know that. But it's such a horrible creature, and he never leaves it alone."

This was true. Antony took Poor Thing everywhere. People in stores smiled at him in a pitying

way, as if he were the Poor Little Match Wretch
. . . or they looked nervous, as if Poor Thing might
spread whatever ghastly misfortunes she'd sur-
vived.

Finally, Aunt said, "We could do something
about that doll."

Antony clutched it tight.

"Wouldn't you like her clean and with two
eyes?"

He shook his head and hugged the doll harder.

"Think how lovely she'd be with hair," Aunt
cajoled.

He backed toward the door, watching Aunt as if
she might go into a doll-napping frenzy at any moment.

"If we could leave her at the doll hospital for just
a day . . ." Aunt murmured.

Antony paused.

"She could have an operation. When she comes
home, we can take her temperature and pulse."
She went on as if that doll would make medical
history. Antony didn't have a chance.

When she won, Aunt telephoned the doll hospital and said it was an emergency.

The next morning, Antony wrapped Poor Thing
in a dish towel and whitened her face with chalk.
When the captain arrived, Antony, grim but game,
carried the patient to the car.

I offered to play catch with Father, but he had to get ready for work.

Aida and I shot baskets. After she made two in a row, I went in to tell Father, but he said, "Got to run."

A little while later, the captain drove up with Aunt, Antony and Poor Thing, who looked just the same.

"The hospital turned her away," Aunt explained. "They said there was no hope."

"THAT DOLL RUINS MY APPETITE." Father glared across the table as Antony pushed French toast between Poor Thing's lips. "From now on, it does not eat with us."

Then Antony lost his appetite.

"I'm worried about my father," I told Sherman that afternoon. "I'm afraid he may take out all his frustrations on Poor Thing some morning."

"Why don't we take the doll and the twins to my house?" Sherman combed Sadie's ears.

"Your house?"

"Sure. My father's not home."

"What about your mother?"

"We'll go in the back door. She never notices what I do, anyway." Sherman put his comb back into his pocket.

I didn't feel comfortable going, but I felt worse hanging around our house with Antony and that doll under my nose, or being seen in public with them.

We trooped up to Sherman's room without being noticed, as he'd promised. We played Chutes and Ladders, the stupid doll taking forever with its turn. One thing led to another, and pretty soon Sherman and I were yelling at it, while Antony held his hands over its ears.

A slender woman with pale skin and green eyes and champagne-colored hair hurried in. "Do I hear harsh voices?"

There was something about her that silenced us instantly. Her clothes were the same color as her hair. Though her voice was soft and breathy, you couldn't imagine anybody arguing with her.

"Now," she said, "shall we have a little pause for reflection and then promise to keep our voices under control?"

Then she noticed Poor Thing, who had gotten flung under Sherman's bed during the yelling. Only an arm and a leg stuck out. "What . . . is that?"

Antony hauled the doll out by a foot.

The woman put a hand to her chest. "Oh."

Antony held the doll tight.

"May I . . . just look at it?" She put out a hand and touched its grubby foot.

Antony jerked as if she'd burned him.

She lifted its moldy cloth arm.

I looked at Sherman. He raised his eyebrows and shrugged.

The woman stared into the blue glass eye. Antony looked as if he expected her to say Poor Thing had only hours to live.

"Whose was it?" she asked.

Antony looked around like a prisoner being interrogated in a foreign tongue.

"Was it your great-grandmama's?" she persisted.

"He adopted it," I said. "From Mr. Troup's garage sale."

The woman slapped her forehead with the heel of her hand. "Garage sale. Garage sale! You picked this up at a *garage sale*?"

I felt as if I'd confessed to garage abuse.

"Oh, my dear!" she cried. "And this little boy drags it around like a *toy*?"

"Just try to get it away from him," I said.

She looked at me a moment, and then turned to my brother. "Darling, do you know what you have there?"

He nodded.

She stroked his knuckles. He stared at his hand.

"What you have there, dear heart, is a perfectly exquisite antique. It must be at least a hundred years old. We have to be very, very careful that it doesn't get any more . . . battered."

Antony looked at her the way Father looks at the mechanic who explains why the car will cost two hundred dollars to repair.

"When a dolly gets this old," the woman crooned, scrabbling closer to my brother on her knees, "she's not to be played with. She's a treasure. *DON'T* squeeze her so tight!" Her voice settled down again. "That cloth is old and weak, and if you squeeze too hard her insides might come out all over the floor."

He looked interested, but she took his arm in a firm grip. "I would give anything for a dolly like that. I would fix her all lovely and put her in a case so everyone could admire her. Wouldn't she be happy?"

As he tried to back away, I took pity on him. "We have to go now."

"May I just hold dolly a moment?" She put out her arms.

As Antony turned to flee, Poor Thing's head hit a chair. Still on her knees, the woman plunged forward. *"Don't damage her!"*

Antony ran.

He was nearly home before Aida and I caught up with him. He dashed into our room, where he huddled for the next hour, hugging Poor Thing.

My father got a telephone call when he got home. He hung up, looking dazed. "That was Mrs.

Grove, about Antony's doll. She says it would be a crime not to restore it. She says it would take weeks of work but she has lined up the artists to do it."

"Antony wouldn't want her so restored he couldn't play with her," Aunt said.

Father looked even more stunned. "Mrs. Grove wants to buy it. She offered me thirty dollars."

I felt uneasy. "What did you tell her?"

"I told her I'd bring it right over."

Aunt and I followed him to my room.

"Guess what?" he greeted Antony.

Antony slid into a corner.

"Mrs. Grove has found somebody who can fix Poor Thing," Father announced.

Antony pulled a pillow off his bed and covered the doll with it.

"How do you think that doll feels being dragged around disgusting everyone?" Father demanded.

"That's not fair," Aunt put in. "Don't play on his guilt feelings."

"This child has no guilt feelings. If he had guilt feelings, he'd speak to me once in a while."

"If you want to sell his doll, tell him," Aunt said. "Don't sneak."

Antony buried his face in the pillow.

"How can I talk to him when he's smothering himself?" Father demanded.

Aunt sat on the floor. "Antony. Sherman's mother will pay thirty dollars for Poor Thing."

"I'll give you ten percent of it," Father told him.

Antony sat up.

We left.

"He can't go on screaming forever," Father said. "Not at that volume."

Aunt was out with Langley Morris when Mrs. Grove called the next day.

"She'll pay fifty dollars for that miserable doll," Father announced.

I followed him to my room.

When my brother saw us, he cringed.

Father sat on the edge of the bed. "Look, Ambrose."

"Antony," I said.

"Antony. Do you know what fifty dollars will buy?"

"He hasn't the foggiest notion," I said. "He's just a kid."

"Don't try to help," Father told me. "Antony, Mrs. Grove will pay fifty dollars for that doll. Imagine how much she must want it."

"We should hold out for seventy-five, then," I said.

Father looked at me as if we'd never met.

He talked to Antony quietly and reasonably.

Antony took a deep breath. He turned blue. Father stood. "All right. I'm going. *Breathe!*"

We didn't have to hold out for seventy-five dollars. Mrs. Grove offered a hundred that evening.

As my father entered my room, Antony crawled under a bed with Poor Thing.

Father got down on hands and knees to explain all the things a hundred dollars would buy.

Antony began to moan.

"It's pretty sad hearing the moans of a five-year-old trapped under a bed by his parent," I said.

Father retreated.

The next morning I grabbed Antony and Aida as soon as the telephone rang. "I'm taking the twins for a walk," I yelled, and ran before anyone could stop us.

In the park some boys chased us, hooting at Antony and insulting his doll.

Suddenly, I'd had all the running I was willing to do. I stopped. I turned. I said, "You are not only dumb, you are stupid. You are not only stupid, you are ignorant. You are not only ignorant, you don't know anything. This doll happens to be an exquisite antique, you twits."

Our tormentors sneered and guffawed, but we all knew I had them outclassed.

"Mrs. Grove, who owns our house, offered a hundred dollars for this antique, and is probably offering more right now." The more I talked, the more furious I got. "If you ever bother my brother again, I will turn my mind to hideous ways to make you suffer unspeakable agonies, until you spend the rest of your miserable lives hiding in fear and terror."

They looked around them and kicked the dirt. One by one, not looking at one another, they strolled away as if they'd just remembered something they had to do somewhere else.

When we got home, Father was gone.

The next morning, he was in a hurry to get to work, but I knew we had only a few hours' respite.

I was wrong.

Not that long.

The telephone rang. Antony slid off his chair.

"We're out," I said.

"I am not going to lie for you, Desdemona Blank," Mrs. Farisee declared.

"By the time you answer the phone, we'll *be* out." Grabbing Antony's hand, I fled with him and Aida and the doll.

As we got to the park, the boys who had chased us hurried away as if they were suddenly late for something important.

After a while one of them drifted back. "Hey. Do you always talk like that?" he asked me.

"Like what?"

"About unspeakable agonies."

"I mean what I say."

"That doll really a squizzled antique?" he asked Antony.

"It's worth a fortune," I said.

The boy sat down and studied it. From a safe distance, one of the others called, "Hey, Merv, you want a dollie?"

Merv stood. "Don't your brother and sister talk?"

"They don't have to."

"Yeah. Well, I got to go beat up a kid." Merv ran after the boy who'd yelled.

I lay under a tree listening to the twins.

"Okay," Aida said. "Poor Thing is the princess and I am the dragon."

"I want to be the dragon," Antony said.

"Okay. I'll be the evil king. The princess is walled up in the tower. Put her in the tree. Okay. Good. The dragon is below the tower, so anybody who comes around gets burned by his breath. I put a spell on, so anybody who gets past him turns into a stupid egg runt."

"Wait a minute." Antony was worried. "Who rescues the princess? I'm the dragon and you're the king and we don't got anybody to save the princess."

"How about Dez?" Aida suggested.

I closed my eyes, knowing I could not sincerely save that doll.

"She doesn't know how to rescue," Antony said.

That hurt, but I kept my eyes shut.

"Well, how about Poor Thing is on a shipwreck?" Aida asked. "She swims to a desert island. The tree can be where she lands. I'm a cannibal and you're a pirate. Dez is the shark. She lies there and swallows people."

"How does Poor Thing get rescued?" Antony asked.

"The shark swallows her," Aida suggested hopefully.

I opened my eyes. "You stop saying things to make him yowl or I'll take you home."

She looked at me. Then she said to Antony, "Okay. Poor Thing lands on a volcano. The which doctors want to throw her in it. The tree can be the volcano. You be a which doctor. I'm a dinosaur that comes crashing through the town just as the volcano explodes."

"What happens to Poor Thing?" He sounded tense.

"She expl—"

I opened one eye.

"She escapes. Only she's carried off by a neegle. The tree is its nest. This giant gorilla comes along."

"YAAAH!"

I sat up.

Merv was waving a cage at us. "YAAAH!"

There was a skinny gray mouse in the cage, hunched and trembling.

I scrambled to my feet. "You rotten kid! How would you like to be locked in a dirty cage with somebody swinging you around?"

"It's my mouse," he muttered.

"That doesn't mean you can lock it up and starve it and torment it!" I yelled.

"Boy." He looked insulted. "How's anybody supposed to make friends with you?" He stomped away, the cage swinging from his hand.

"That poor mouse. Poor thing." I was so sad and angry I had to work not to cry.

Antony clutched my hand.

I took a deep breath. "I'm okay. Listen—why don't I fix some sandwiches, and we'll have a picnic where nobody will bother us."

He held my hand tight all the way home.

I left him and Aida in the back yard with the dogs while I went in to make our lunch.

To my relief, Mrs. Farisee was out. Aunt was repairing the hinges of a kitchen cupboard.

"I'm going to make a lunch and take the twins out again in case Mrs. Grove keeps calling," I told her.

She nodded.

"This is more serious than just the doll," I said. "You know how Antony loves it."

"Oh, yes." She put down the screwdriver.

"You know how Mrs. Grove wants it. I'm wondering if she wants it enough to persuade her husband to let us stay here."

"Good point."

"Am I talking about blackmail?" I asked anxiously.

"Blackmail is entirely different. You're talking about hard bargaining in a good cause."

"Antony would give up the doll to keep the dogs." My throat felt tight, as if it didn't want to let the words out. "I know he would. It's just . . . It's pretty rotten when one little kid has to do all the giving up."

"I know."

"I guess I have to ask him. Then how do I put a tough bargain to a lady like Mrs. Grove?"

"You do the hard part. Ask Antony to give up his doll. Then I'll ask Mrs. Grove to deal with her husband. I'll help you fix the picnic now."

When I went out with our lunch there was no sign of the twins. They weren't allowed to go anywhere alone. I looked out front, and around the block, and when I came back to the house they weren't there, so Aunt and I went different directions looking.

The third time I returned, Mrs. Farisee was in the kitchen.

"What do you mean by leaving your brother and sister here all alone?" she demanded.

"Nobody left them. They left us."

She called them into the kitchen and reprimanded them. I raged at them. In the middle of my tirade, Aunt came home and told them they were never to do such a stupid, thoughtless thing again.

Nobody told my father the twins had run off; I think we all figured they'd had enough dumped on them for one day.

In the middle of dinner the telephone rang. As Father stood, the rest of us hunched our shoulders and looked at our plates.

When he hung up he looked haggard. "One hundred fifty."

"Not now," Aunt said. "Not at the table."

I was drying dishes when the doorbell rang. Father went to the door.

I heard Mrs. Grove's voice. Sherman hurried into the kitchen. "That woman never gives up." He went to my room to warn Antony, then came running back to tell me what Antony had.

I hurried to my room to see. A minute later, Mrs. Grove swept in.

"How is my little friend?"

Antony backed against the wall, one hand inside his shirt.

Mrs. Grove knelt in front of him. "Do you know how much money two hundred dollars is? Stop scratching your tummy. You could buy a nice bike with that money."

Behind her, Father said, "Or several pairs of shoes. Or a few visits to the dentist."

"Two hundred dollars is more than some boys get in allowance in a whole year," she said.

"Much more," Father said firmly. "Stop scratching your chest, Antony."

Mrs. Grove seized Antony's free hand. "Don't you want Sherman's mommy to be happy? The one thing that would make me happier than anything in the world would be to take dolly and make her beautiful."

Antony looked at me. It was a plea.

"Um . . . I'm not sure he still has that doll," I ventured.

Father seized my shoulders. "What do you mean?"

"I have a feeling Poor Thing may be with some kid we met in the park."

Pale and wide-eyed, Antony nodded.

Father and Mrs. Grove bombarded me with questions. Remembering how prisoners of war were expected to behave, all I told them was the boy's name and size and where I'd last seen him.

"Why in the world would a twelve-year-old male delinquent want the disgusting thing?" Father was dazed. "Why would any nut want that old doll?"

Mrs. Grove leveled a long look at him.

Not even a prisoner of war could stand up to the pressure she and he exerted. I promised to help find the boy, and they went to the parlor.

I shut my door, and Sherman and Aida and I sat on the floor. As Antony drew his hand out from under his shirt, the mouse scampered up his arm. Settling on his shoulder, it washed its face fastidiously with its paws.

I told Sherman how Merv had abused it.

"Poor thing." Sherman stroked it gently.

"You're a weird kid," I told my brother, "but you're a good person."

Before I could defend myself, he hugged me.

After Sherman and his mother left, I told the twins, "Someone has to break the mouse news."

They looked at me.

"We can't keep a mouse secret forever."

Their eyes were full of trust.

I took two glasses of lemonade to the parlor. "I thought you might like to talk."

Father stared at his glass. "Why would he just give the doll away? He loved it—loved it more than a hundred dollars."

"Would you rather have your children kind or rich? And don't say kind of rich."

He looked at me, dull-eyed.

After I made him swear to be calm and under-standing, I took him back to my room.

The mouse was cuddled on Aida's shoulder.

"This was a poor thing, too," I said.

Father still didn't understand. "Poor Thing Two?"

"This mouse, this poor skinny mouse, was dragged around in a tiny dirty cage by a rotten kid. You can see it's been through a lot."

"Oh, no." Father sounded the way he did when I told him the dogs ate his paycheck. "He—"

"Traded Poor Thing for this poor thing." I put my arm around Father. "You should be proud of your son."

As I led him away, he was muttering, ". . . two-hundred-dollar mouse . . ."

SO ANTONY DESTROYED ANY HOPE of trading the doll for our staying in the house. Even if Mrs. Grove got the doll, now, it would be from Merv. I was terrified that she'd find Merv and learn Antony had the mouse. I was sure the Groves would not be tolerant about a mouse living in any house they owned.

For a while, I thought about finding Merv, getting the doll from him, and trading it to Mrs. Grove for canceling our eviction, but I realized that, unless Merv were very weird, he only took the doll because I'd said it was worth a fortune. I had twenty-six cents, a battered girl's bike, and a pair of run-down roller skates to offer a tough street kid for a priceless antique.

Blank's Law again.

From what I'd seen of Mrs. Grove, I knew she would find Merv with or without my help.

Early the next morning, Sherman came to our back door.

"Tell him he's not allowed over here before breakfast," Mrs. Farisee ordered.

I went to the door.

"My mother's going to telephone you any minute," Sherman whispered. "She's getting ready to go to the park with you and find the boy who has Poor Thing."

"I'm going to the park with Sherman," I called. "I'll be back."

As Sherman and I hurried away, I knew I was in big trouble. I'd run off without permission, without breakfast, and without doing my chores—but I had to get to Merv before Mrs. Grove did.

"Where are we going?" Sherman panted.

I didn't have the breath to explain.

When we got to the park, I saw Merv's friends playing football—mostly knocking each other around and arguing.

I hurried toward them.

Sherman slowed down. "They're awfully big, and rough."

As Merv's friends saw me coming, they stopped yelling. They looked at one another and looked away and then all hurried off in different directions, heads down.

"Hey!" I yelled. "I want to talk to you!"

They ran.

"Wow!" Sherman gasped. "What did you do to them?"

It was midmorning before we came upon Merv sitting alone, throwing rocks at a sign that said RESPECT YOUR PARK. When he saw me, he stood. "You stay away."

"Listen," I said, "I have to talk to you."

"Talk! Your talk rooned my life. Everybody made so much fun of me and that doll, I hid it. Then my mother and father found it. They don't listen. My father don't even want me around the house." He looked more glum. " 'Course, he never did."

"Desdemona!"

Without turning, Sherman cringed. "I should have known. There is no escaping that woman."

"Merv," I said quickly, "when Mrs. Grove gets here, don't say a word about the mouse, understand? Not a word about the mouse!"

"There you are." I felt a soft hand on my shoulder. "I'm glad I found you, Desdemona. Are you ready to go look for Merv?"

Merv gazed at her, blond and scented, soft-voiced, her silky dress matching her eyes. "Hey," he rasped, "there really is a Mrs. Grove?"

She looked at him as if he were something rejected by her trash collector. "Who are you?"

"Merv," he muttered.

"Merv!" she breathed. "Merv, where is the doll Antony Blank gave you?"

"Nobody *give* me. I traded for it."

"Mrs. Grove wants that doll," I said hastily.

"Boy, does she want it," Sherman said.

Merv's father was watching television when we burst into his kitchen. "Look!" Merv chortled, "There *is* a Mrs. Grove! Where's that doll?"

Putting down the beer can, Merv's father stood, smoothing his undershirt and feeling for his slippers with his feet.

"She'll pay a fortune for it," I said, to reassure him.

Mrs. Grove put a hand on my shoulder, firmly. "You wait outside."

"She'll pay anything for it," Sherman added.

"Take him with you." Her lips barely moved.

Sitting on the fire escape, we could hear her talking louder than I'd ever dreamed she could. When she came out, brushing coffee grounds and spaghetti strands off the doll, she muttered, "That man is a robber."

Merv's father came out after her. "Nice doing business with you, lady. I hope the other little boy likes Merv's mouse."

"Why don't we get going," I urged.

She turned. "Mouse? What mouse?"

"The one Merv traded him for your doll."

I was right. Mrs. Grove had no softness in her heart for a mouse. I went home with her ultimatum echoing in my ears.

Mrs. Farisee had already discovered the mouse. Her ultimatum was even shorter and sharper than Mrs. Grove's. "It goes or I go."

The twins were innocent enough to think we had a choice.

Mrs. Farisee called my father at work, and when she finished speaking to him, handed me the receiver. His voice was so loud the twins, at my side, heard and trembled.

We sat in our room, watching the mouse scramble up the curtains and slide down, until Aunt came home.

The minute I heard the captain's car, I raced to the front door. "We've got a terrible problem," I told him and Aunt.

"I've never known you to have another kind," he observed.

"Has anybody told you about the mouse?"

"Mouse?" she asked. *Mouse?*

I told them about it and about the ultimatums from Mrs. Grove and Mrs. Farisee and my own father.

"People don't understand that a mouse, properly brought up, is a lovely, bright, gentle animal." Aunt looked at the captain. "Really, Langley."

"I have a feeling I am going to learn to appreciate one. Desdemona, do you want to bring my new mouse to meet me?"

When Antony and Aida brought it out, it looked at him with shy mouse eyes. "The first thing," he said, "is to get you out of that miserable little cage into decent quarters, and then get you properly fed."

A few days later, Sherman and I saw Merv at the park carrying a mitt and softball.

"See you at the field," Merv told his friends.

"Okay, Merv."

"Sure, Merv."

"See you, Merv."

He walked along with Sherman and me for a while. "Boy, that Mrs. Grove."

Sherman nodded. "Yeah."

"I got this ball and mitt and some new clothes."

"You even look cleaner," I observed.

"I say 'What time is it?' my father answers me now. I say 'When we gonna eat?' my mother tells me when, even what. I got a uncle says when I'm growed I should go into business. The guys treat me like some kind of star, you know?"

"That's nice," I murmured.

"Eeh." Merv kicked a rock. "I feel like some-body else."

"I guess it's lonely at the top," Sherman said.

SINCE MRS. GROVE HAD gotten the doll from Merv's father, there was no way to bargain with her about letting us stay. Days went by with no sign of a place we could live with our dogs.

Sherman was almost as upset as my father. "What are we going to do about the dogs if no place will have them?"

He tried talking to his parents. According to him, they didn't notice.

One morning he came over and told me, "I've changed my name."

"What's wrong with Sherman?"

"My parents chose it."

"What's your new name?"

"Houlihan."

"Houlihan Grove?"

"Spike Houlihan."

"Who do you know named Houlihan?"

"Nobody. That's why I picked it."

A few days later, the milkman brought Spike along with our morning delivery. "They found this kid in with the cows. I see him at the Grove house all the time, but he says he don't mix with that bunch. When I started to take him to the police station, he said you could identify him."

"We'll take him," I said.

After the milkman left Spike and our order, I got stern. "Leaving home won't solve anything, Houlihan."

"If they notice when I'm gone, they may notice when I'm not."

"Go home. I'm going to call your house in twenty minutes, and if you're not there I'll never let you see the dogs again."

He left. When I telephoned, he answered.

"Did you get in trouble?" I asked.

"Nobody knew I was missing. Mr. Grove has left for work and Mrs. Grove is still asleep. Their maid looked at the dirt in my hair and said I shouldn't play at your house so much."

A few mornings later, the zoo in Maundy Park called. A Spike Houlihan had gotten into the monkey island somehow and refused to give a home address. When the keeper threatened him, he gave our telephone number.

I had the keeper bring Spike to the telephone. I gave Spike ninety minutes to get home.

When I called his house, he answered.

"Your parents won't stand for this," I said.

"Who?"

"Mr. and Mrs. Grove."

"Mrs. Grove is at her judo lesson. Mr. Grove is golfing. Their maid said I'm not to play at your place anymore. She said I smelled like a zoo."

Langley Morris invited us all to his farm for the Fourth of July so the dogs wouldn't have to put up with firecrackers.

When I called to tell Sherman, he felt terrible. "My parents are sending me to summer camp because our maid quit." He was silent a minute. "When you're sent away from home, there's no point left in leaving home."

Mrs. Farisee went to her sister's for the Fourth, and my father kept looking at houses.

"It needs work," the captain admitted as the rest of us got to the farm.

He was right.

"You know," Aunt said thoughtfully, "a good tiller could work those weeds right into the ground. They'd make good fertilizer, and it's not too late to plant some winter crops."

"She's also great at repairing knobs and hinges,"

I told the captain. Then I was afraid I might encourage him to woo her away from us.

The dogs found the farm just fine as it was. They rushed over to greet Moriarty and work out a chasing game with him. Baskerville sat well out of reach, watching with tolerant disdain.

Antony and Aida went in to visit the mouse, who'd become sleek and fearless, running up our arms to inspect our hair and nuzzle our ears.

Outside, there was a barking, a surging through the weeds, and then all the dogs leaped at the fence.

"Sherman!" I ran out of the mouse room.

When he finished rolling around with the dogs, I asked, "How did you get here?"

He grinned.

"Did you hitchhike?" the captain asked sternly.

"No, sir," Sherman said. "I used my snack allowance for bus fares."

"I see you brought your backpack," the captain said.

"And my sleeping bag. You don't have to go to any trouble."

Aunt looked at Sherman closely. "Do your parents know you're here?"

"The camp has probably notified them of my absence."

Aunt went in and telephoned his house.

"It was good of you to leave a note at camp

addressed to Mr. and Mrs. Grove," she said when she came back, "but they're a bit hurt that you call them 'To Whom It May Concern.'"

"Where shall I put my stuff?" he asked the captain.

"You could have told them something more than that you were going to live with friends," Aunt persisted.

"I'll only stay until I get my future planned," Sherman assured the captain.

"You'll only stay until tomorrow," she said. "Your parents would come for you now, but your father has to make a speech at a Fourth of July picnic." She looked at Langley Morris. "His parents are going to a dinner party this evening, and they say it's too late to find a sitter."

After we ate, we started building a tree house in a giant oak behind the barn. Aunt and the captain secured a platform to the branches, then Sherman and I nailed up walls. The captain found sheets of plywood for a roof. Aunt made a door with scrap wood and old hinges from a shed, and Sherman found a rusty dead bolt near the hinges. The twins handed up pine cones and bark and a good supply of mud cakes.

After the rest of us were finished, Sherman kept working on the tree house.

"Come on," I yelled up at him. "It's supposed to be fun, not work."

He came down for dinner. The captain said that since Sherman was spending the night, the rest of us should come back the next day to enjoy the tree house.

We were all up early the next morning. "The captain invited us back to his farm," I told my father. "Are you going to come?"

He shook his head. "With four weeks in which to find a place to live? I'm down to looking at buildings I wouldn't have considered fit for a kennel last year."

He drove us to the farm and went on, looking so tired I was tempted to run after his car.

The captain met us at the gate and handed Aunt a note, which she read and passed to me:

> *Dear captain, I have borrowed some food. I am leaving you my transistor radio. Tell the Groves I will contact them when I am adult about what to do with my other belongings.*

"We have to find him!" I cried.

"I found him," the captain said.

Sherman had pulled the ladder up after him into the tree house, one end sticking out of the slit he'd left for a window.

"I'd better call his parents," Aunt said.

It is hard to enjoy a visit when one of the guests is silent up in a tree.

It was impossible to enjoy anything when Mr. Grove arrived. It was the first time we'd seen him since he told us to move, and he seemed as uncomfortable as any of us.

"Where?" he asked.

The captain pointed at the tree house.

"Sherman, it's time to go," Mr. Grove said.

"Sherman," he called, "I'll be late for my tennis date."

Then, "Sherman?"

And, "Sherman, stop being silly and come down here."

Again, "Sherman, I am ordering you to come down!"

Mr. Grove yelled at Sherman until his voice got raspy. "I'd climb up there, but I don't see any way to get a foothold," he told the captain.

"He's bolted the door from the inside," the captain said.

"It seems to me," Aunt observed, "it might help if you find out why he's done it."

Mr. Grove cleared his throat. "I wonder if you could tell me," he shouted politely at the tree house, "why you want to live in a tree rather than with your mother and me."

"Better say 'the Groves,'" I suggested.

He ignored me, but when there was no sound from above, he asked, "What have you got against the Groves, Sherman?"

Silence.

"I think he feels you don't pay attention to him," I ventured.

Mr. Grove ignored me. "Sherman, answer!"

Nothing.

"Is it because we don't pay enough attention to you?" he yelled at the tree.

Quiet.

Then, from the tree house, "Yeah."

"Oh."

"Also because you're making us move," I said.

"Is it also because I'm making the Blanks move?"

A pause, then, "Yeah."

"All right, Sherman. Come down and we'll talk about letting them stay. All right? Fair enough? Sherman?"

I thought of some other things that would upset me if I were Sherman, and Mr. Grove asked him about them and Sherman said yeah. He didn't come down, though.

"Sherman," his father shouted, "I cannot stand down here all day finding out why you're determined to live in a tree. You cannot live in a tree. It's unsanitary. Do you want me to have that tree cut down?"

The captain gave Mr. Grove a long, hard look.

I told Mr. Grove about Sherman at the dairy and the zoo.

"Don't you see what the boy is trying to tell you?" Aunt asked him.

He looked exhausted. "He's not sure he's human?"

"That boy is lonely," she said. "Why do you suppose he spends all his time with us? Your son needs love and companionship."

Mr. Grove was silent. Then he lifted his voice. "All right, Sherman. I'll buy you a dog."

There was a long pause, then a scraping noise. The ladder was pushed out the window until one end rested on the ground. The door opened.

Sherman backed down the ladder.

The captain's voice was low. "In a way, I hate to see him surrender."

THE SUSPENSE WAS SO HIGH none of us dared talk about it, except Father. "Don't get your heart set on staying," he warned me. "Sherman's father was acting under pressure."

When we didn't hear from any Grove for three days, I could stand it no more. I telephoned Sherman.

"How have you been?" I couldn't bring myself to come right out and ask if we could stay.

"All right." His voice sounded flat and faraway.

"Sherman, are you sick?"

"No."

"Uh . . . well . . . are you going to get a dog?"

"I did."

"Hey! Bring it over!"

"I've got to go, Dez." He hung up.

"Something is very, very wrong," I told Aunt. "I have to see Sherman."

When I knocked at the back door of his house, I heard something that sounded like a deranged hamster inside.

A maid let me in.

What looked like the head of a dustmop bounced at my feet, squeaking savagely, jiggling and jittering on tippy claws. It was a yap dog, all hair and all white, except for its pink-painted nails. ·

"Shermahn," the maid called. "Come feed your dog."

Sherman trudged into the kitchen as if his bones ached. Without looking at me, he poured the contents of a foil packet into a pink bowl with PRECIOUS stenciled on it.

As Sherman set the bowl on the floor, the yap dog backed away, yipping.

"Well." I tried to keep my voice neutral. "If it's not hungry, we can take it out to play."

Still Sherman didn't look at me. "He just had a bath. My father doesn't want him to get dirty."

"We could carry him to my house."

"My father says your place is probably full of fleas."

"Sherman, who picked this dog?"

"Who do you think?"

I hesitated, but then I had to end the suspense one way or another. "Did you talk about letting us stay in our house?"

"Sure. We talked. He told me all the reasons why you still have to leave."

I didn't see Sherman again until the Founder's Day picnic at Bear Creek Canyon.

I wanted to take our dogs, but my father said there was no way to get them and us into one car.

"Aunt's going with Langley Morris. The twins and I could ride with them, so you'd have just Mrs. Farisee and yourself. Two people and three dogs would fit."

"Three people. I'm bringing a friend. I doubt if she'd enjoy sharing a ride with three dogs who go manic in a car, not to mention their tendency to get carsick."

"Did you ask your friend if *she* gets carsick?"

"I'm not going to take any sarcasm from you," he told me firmly. "Besides, if the dogs wandered from the picnic area into the woods, we'd have a devil of a time finding them."

The twins and I rode with Aunt and the captain anyway, so I didn't meet my father's friend until we all got to Bear Creek Canyon. Father introduced her as Shirley. She looked about thirty, and considerably less flashy than I expected—but of course a picnic is not an occasion for flash.

The picnic area was a few dusty acres between the road and the wood, dotted with a couple of dozen tables and firepits.

The Groves and other City Council members and families had a table in front of a small stage decked with red, white and blue bunting.

We took a table to their left and a little behind them.

The high school band on the stage played "The Washington Post March" and "Stars and Stripes Forever" loudly and sincerely, while people set out Thermos jugs and hampers. Soon the air was hazy from cooking fires, and little kids were clamoring for the soft drinks at the Rotary Club stand, and it seemed to me that every other family there had two parents.

After the City Council members filed onto the stage the Mayor made a speech. Mr. Grove got a Junior Chamber of Commerce award. Accepting it, he talked about the meaning of Founder's Day, and how every American was entitled to honest wages and food and shelter.

"Is it all right if the twins and I play ball?" I whispered.

My father nodded.

I took Antony and Aida and our softball to a clearing between the picnic area and the trees. The twins were pretty good at catching. "Wait here," I told them. "I'll go get our mitt."

Mr. Grove was saying, "I want to introduce the lovely lady without whom . . ." Handing Precious to Sherman, Mrs. Grove walked to the stage while Sherman struggled to keep the dog quiet and off the table and out of the potato chips.

As I started back to the twins, Precious wriggled free and darted toward the trees. Clutching the bag of chips, Sherman ran after him.

Aida and Antony were tossing the ball back and forth when the dog leaped between them and grabbed it. I don't know how he got his jaws around it, but he managed. He dashed toward the trees, Sherman and the twins after him.

I followed. Five minutes into the woods, everything around me was cool and dim, the sunlight gone. Somewhere ahead were sounds of twigs cracking and branches whipping.

"Hey!" I yelled. "Come back here!" As the noise veered to the right, I changed course.

Finally I saw something move ahead of me. "Hold still!" I called.

It did. Catching up, I saw it was Sherman.

"Which way did they go?" I asked.

"I don't know."

We could hear faint sounds, but it was hard to tell from where.

"We've got to find them!" Sherman groaned. "That dog cost money!"

As we followed the sounds, it occurred to me

that we should mark our trail. "Maybe we could scatter potato chips, like Hansel and Gretel . . . but what if foraging beasts ate them?"

"Who? Ate who?" he quavered.

"The chips," I reassured him. Then I wondered if potato chips might *attract* foraging beasts. "What kind of animals hang around these parts?"

"Don't talk about it." He clutched the chip sack against his chest.

As we went on, the woods grew darker, hushed, the trees taller and more dense.

"Dez." Sherman's voice trembled. "We have to separate. There are three of them to find and only two of us."

Too nervous to question his reasoning, I looked around us. "See that tree? It's taller than the rest. If you find them, or even if you start to get tired, get back to that tree. I'll go for help."

I started back for the picnic area, trying to find every odd rock and stump I'd noted before.

Ahead of me, I heard crashing in the brush. My heart skittering wildly, I made myself yell, "Hey!"

I almost walked into the twins, scared and scratched and very glad to see me.

"Where's the dog?"

They shrugged.

I made Aida hold Antony's hand tight, and I held hers and led them on.

The landmarks I remembered seemed to have

vanished, and I was remembering stories about lost patrols wandering in circles to their doom, when I heard cheers; distant cheers, but cheers. We headed for them.

Through the trees, I saw the picnic area, and a baseball game on our side of the tables. As we straggled out of the wood, my father hurried to us. "I've been looking all over. Where the devil did you go?"

"After Sherman's dog and your children."

"Where's Sherman?"

"Under a tree."

"You *left* him?"

"I thought you might want your children back."

Mrs. Grove came toward us. "Desdemona, have you seen—"

"Your dog ran into the woods and he went after it," I told her.

Father beckoned to Shirley, who was about to pitch. Handing the ball to somebody else, she loped over to us, followed by Aunt and Langley Morris.

"I'm going to take the twins to Mrs. Farisee," Father told them. "Sherman is somewhere in the woods."

By the time I finished explaining to Mrs. Grove what had happened, my father was back with Mr. Grove.

We had to get well into the woods before I could

spot the tall tree, but once I saw it we got to it without much trouble. Sherman wasn't there.

"Someone should wait here," Father said, "while the rest look around, just to be on the safe side. Who has a watch?"

He and the Groves and Langley Morris did.

"We'll meet here in an hour," Father said.

Mr. Grove stayed at the tree. Father and Shirley and I went one way, and the captain and Aunt and Mrs. Grove another.

Vast and dim, the woods seemed less threatening with my father near me.

"Got a knife on you?" Shirley asked him.

He handed her his Swiss Army knife.

Taking off her sweater, she cut it and started unraveling the yarn. As we walked among the trees, shouting for Sherman, she tied bits of yarn onto branches.

"Let's call the dog for a change," Father suggested finally.

"Precious!" I yelled.

Shirley winced. "Poor thing."

Father and I looked at each other. "Poor thing?" he asked.

"Poor dog to be stuck with a name like Precious and poor kid to be stuck with a dog named Precious."

I was forced to admit that Shirley had sense.

We scrambled over stumps and around poison

oak, and at the end of an hour we were back with Aunt and the Groves and the captain.

"There's no point struggling back here every hour," Langley Morris said. "Let's meet here in two." He looked at the Groves, who were pale and tense. "Why don't you go back to the picnic and round up more help?"

Mrs. Grove shook her head. "I want to wait here."

While Aunt stayed with her, Mr. Grove headed back to the picnic area, Father and Shirley and I went a different way, and the captain went still another.

We'd been walking and yelling for almost an hour when things began to get lively.

We ran into Mr. Troup and the Mayor calling, "Sherman." Then we came across a reporter with a photographer who asked us to stand still and look alert but concerned. A few minutes later, we encountered Mr. Grove and three Eagle Scouts.

Shirley and Father and I went on deeper into the woods. There was only the crunching of leaves underfoot. Then the crunching changed. I looked down at my feet.

"Potato chips! *Sherman!*" Climbing on the fallen trunk of an enormous old tree, I looked down into a gulley. Sherman was sitting in a fall of leaves. Several feet from him, Precious danced around a bush, yipping wildly. The potato chip bag was caught in the bush.

Beside me, my father peered into the gulley. "Are you all right?"

"No." Sherman's voice was strained.

"It's a steep incline, and the ground's wet and slippery. How do we get down there?" Shirley asked Sherman.

"I don't know," he said. "I tripped over the stupid dog and fell in."

"Give me your shirt and jacket," Shirley told Father. She tied them and my cardigan together by the sleeves and gave Father one end. Holding the other, she slid down the side of the gulley, then let go and jumped the last few feet.

"Where do you hurt?" she asked Sherman.

"My ankle."

"Anyplace else?"

He shook his head.

"I'm going to boost you as high as I can, so you can grab the end of the sleeve hanging there."

It worked. My father pulled Sherman up. Precious was another matter. He danced around Shirley, yapping, until she took the chip bag out of the bush. Crumbling it, she pitched it up to me, and the dog managed to scramble his way right out of the gulley, after it. Then my father hauled Shirley up.

When we got back to Mrs. Grove, she held Sherman with her face buried in his hair, not speaking.

"Fantastic! Hold it!" The reporter came through the trees, followed by the photographer.

While Shirley and my father went for Mr. Grove, the reporter asked us questions and the photographer tried to snap pictures without getting nipped by Precious.

Father and Shirley behind him, Mr. Grove came running and grabbed his wife and son, tears streaming down his face.

"Could we get a shot of the rescuers with the parents and the dog?" asked the photographer. "What's the dog's name?"

Sherman lifted his head. "Jake."

"What a story!" The reporter beamed. *"Hero Dog Leads Rescuers to Councilman's Lost Child."*

"Then how about *Lost Child's Father Evicts Rescuers?"* Aunt suggested.

"Despite Lost Child's Pleas," I added.

"Joke. Just a joke." Taking my father's arm, Mr. Grove led him aside.

The newspaper story described how "Jake" had guarded Sherman and led us to him.

"The only leading that dog did," I told Aunt, "was leading Sherman and the twins astray. He tripped Sherman into the gulley, and he didn't guard anything but potato chips." I thought it over a minute. "If it weren't for old Jake, though, we'd still be looking for a place to live."

I think Sherman started to believe the newspaper account. Looking brave and noble, he hobbled around letting people admire his hero dog. The dog even seemed to change, maybe because he was treated like a serious canine. He followed Sherman, looking aloof but tolerant when people complimented him.

AUNT AND LANGLEY MORRIS had a small wedding.

"It's not because you're afraid of Mr. Troup, is it?" I asked her.

"Not really. I'm just terrified of retribution," she confessed.

The ceremony was surprisingly calm. One of the dogs had gnawed the sleeve of the bride's gown, so it was a little slobbery. Having Antony for a ring bearer was a mistake. He stuck the ring on his thumb and, when it was time to give it to the captain, tried to pry it off with his teeth. Mrs. Grove whacked him on the back just in time to save him from swallowing it, and I grabbed him just as he started removing his shoes.

Otherwise, it was as happy and festive as Aunt

said weddings should be. Only, after she and the captain drove away, I wanted to cry.

That night, after the twins were asleep, I did, the dogs sitting on me, kissing me and trying to shake hands.

My father came in. "Why don't you get dressed, and we'll go get something to eat."

He took me to the drive-in where the captain and Aunt and the cat and I had eaten the night of Pat Troup's wedding.

"I don't know what's wrong with me," I told him. "I don't even know why I feel sad."

"You may feel as if you've lost Aunt, but we haven't. You'll visit her all the time. You'll have a genuine Aunt farm."

"I'm even sorry Mrs. Farisee said she had a headache and didn't come to the wedding. I keep imagining how she must feel, caring for a house that's not hers and kids she doesn't much like. Why am I making myself miserable like this?"

"Weddings do that. They're poignant . . . reminders . . . of other events, other weddings."

I knew I could never tell him how sorry I felt for him. When I could talk, I asked, "When you lose somebody, does it ever stop hurting?"

"It lets up. They say that after a while, there's just a twinge now and then."

"How long does that take?"

"I don't know."

"Are we an awful burden, the twins and I?"

He smiled. "Sometimes you're awful, sometimes a burden. I couldn't bear not having you."

"Will she ever come back?"

"Your mother? I don't know. I don't know if it would work now, even if she did."

"Do you ever think about getting married again?"

"Not often."

"To Shirley?"

"No. I like her, but that's all."

"She's a good sign, though. She shows your taste is maturing."

He laughed.

"What will we do if Antony and Aida don't have more to say when they start school?" I wondered.

"Worry."

"I read once that Einstein didn't talk at all until he was four or five . . . or was it Edison? What the heck, my hair came back, didn't it?"

"You have no idea how much I love you," he said.

ABOUT THE AUTHOR

"I'm in the world of the book when I'm writing," says Beverly Keller. During these times, she doesn't go to the store or clean house, and she lives on crackers and peanut butter. However, her six dogs continue to enjoy a majestic lifestyle, with regular meals and care. In this apparently haphazard fashion, Beverly Keller has created many laugh-aloud books, including *Desdemona— Twelve Going on Desperate*, also available in a Harper Trophy edition.